SAVE THE SEA

Beth
Win the
crown.

g Bailey

Save the Sea

Saved by Pirates series

G. Bailey

Other Books by G. Bailey

A Demon's Fall Series

The Familiar Empire Series

From The Stars Series

The Forest Pack Series

The Secret Gods Prison Series

The Rejected Mate Series

Fall Mountain Shifters Series

Royal Reapers Academy Series

The Everlasting Curse Series

SEVEN SEAS and SEVEN ISLANDS

Cover design by Amaliach book cover design

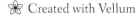 Created with Vellum

Love. Death. Power. When all these words are marked on Cassandra's soul, can she really save anyone?

Cassandra has finally escaped the king, only to find herself in the middle of the rebels and a war that she is meant to be the leader of. When the changed ones of the mountains go to war, Cassandra and her pirates have to travel across the seas to the mermaids who are the only ones that can help.

But what is the price of the mermaids' help?

War is whispered, much like the Sea god whispers to Cassandra, but no one speaks the ending.

Can death be the only winner?

For those who souls belong to the sea.

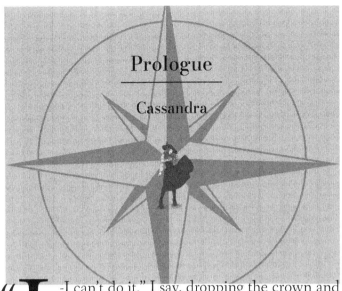

Prologue

Cassandra

"-I can't do it," I say, dropping the crown and dagger onto the floor, staying still as they bounce on the wood before settling. The sounds of dragons roaring, swords smashing against each other, and screams can be heard outside. Yet, the room is eerily silent in a way. Queen Riah keeps her eyes locked with mine, not blinking, not moving. She is like a doll, no fear showing in her eyes as I face her with a dagger. Not even when it is clear that I came here to kill her. Her lips mumble something, but it's nothing that I can make out as actual words. I watch her lean down and picking up the crown, a glow floating up her arms.

"You must let me die. You have to save the future, you have to save the sea, Cassandra," she insists. It's the most I've ever heard her speak. Maybe the crown is giving her some power that she is able to use to speak to me normally. To be able to get past the damage that has been done to her by a man she once loved and trusted.

"You're their mother, and I *love* them. I can't do this to them," I say, taking a deep breath. While I need to be strong, to be emotionless, I'm not. I can't do this, and it will cost me everything.

"You love my sons. They are your chosen," she says, and looks down at the crown for a long while. I don't answer her, she knows the answer, anyway.

"They are fighting the king now, with my other chosen and my army. They don't know I'm here, or what I came to do," I explain to her, hating that I had to make this decision without them. *And I still couldn't do it.*

"They wouldn't stop you. It's time that I died, and you will be able to send my evil chosen after me. I will make sure he pays in death. His soul will burn with the god of souls in hell," she exclaims, and I believe her completely. I can see the determination in her eyes. She looks up, her eyes so much like Ryland's as she smiles when her mouth parts in shock. She coughs, blood trickling out of her mouth, and I look down to see the end of a long dagger jutting through her stomach.

"Finally, I get to be with my chosen," she murmurs as the dagger is pulled out. "Not that they ever really left me," she whispers as the light in her eyes fades, and her soul leaves her body. She falls suddenly, and I catch her, holding her to me as I look up and see who has killed the queen.

"You . . . . How could it be you?"

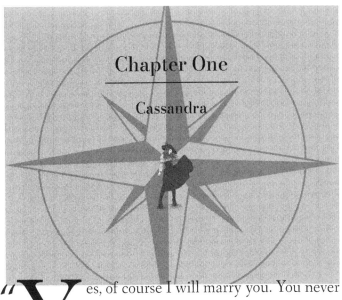

Chapter One

Cassandra

"Yes, of course I will marry you. You never even had to ask. I've belonged to each one of you from the moment you saved me," I say, watching as each of their faces light up. Hunter slides the ring onto my finger before he pulls me into his arms. I bury my face in his neck, sliding my arms around him as he holds me close. I breathe in his familiar scent, loving how I feel so safe in his arms, so right. He holds me tightly, almost like he never wants to let me go, and to be honest, I don't want him to either. Hunter pulls back a little, smoothing his hands over my scar-free arms, with enough emotion swirling in his dark eyes that I never want to look away. I do, though, only for a second to take in his appearance, and how much one year has changed him. His hair is longer than before, hitting his chest. It's smooth and dark, with the familiar feather back in its rightful place. Hunter has grown a slight beard, which makes him look older and meaner, but the love in his eyes reminds me that the most important thing hasn't changed. I can feel my bond with all of them spark up inside of me, feeling alive with happiness at being so close to them all. I glance around quickly at my other chosen, seeing each of them watching me with content and happy looks. There's a longing between us, but more for them as so much time has passed for them. It doesn't feel like we have left the castle, and all its night-mares, all that long ago for me. *How did they make it a whole year without knowing where I was?* If it was the other way around, I don't think I could do it. I would lose my mind, I would drown the world to find them. They are my loves, my chosen, my pirates, and soon will be my husbands.

"How are you healed? It doesn't make sense. I saw my father throw a fireball at you. You shouldn't look like this," Hunter asks, snapping me back from my thoughts and back to my pirates. I look at my pale arms, scar-less and perfect, and part of me hates to see my skin like this. It makes it seem like my life has been perfect, flawless, and it's not been. If anything, I love the flaws in my life, they've shown what I have survived. Reminded me what I need to fight for. There was a beauty to the scars I had, a beauty that shows I survived.

"The sea god healed me, but I don't know how. I woke up like this," I admit as he pulls me back to him, surrounding me with his warm scent. I feel him slide his hands through my long hair, just as I bury my face near his neck. I see his purple feather out of the corner of my eye, and it reminds me of home. Our home, my pirates, and everything we will have to fight for now. The king wouldn't have been sitting around doing nothing for this last year, and that means he will have been planning this whole time. He could be better prepared than us. Even thinking of the king sends shivers through me.

"Then I have him to thank, not that the scars changed a thing about you, but you never should have had them. I missed you, little bird," he says quietly, but every word is filled with emotion, his voice cracking as he calls me by the nickname he always has. How funny it is that the nickname I hated–that I never understood why he called me it– makes me so happy now.

"Why do you call me little bird?" I ask quietly.

It's strange; I know there are so many people in the room, but it is so quiet. So peaceful and silent.

"When I first saw you, you looked like a little bird that wanted to fly away, but I didn't want to let you go," he says, and I feel a hand on my shoulder.

"We all agree with never wanting to let her go, brother," Ryland says, and Hunter reluctantly releases his hold on me. I turn to see Chaz and Ryland right next to me, both watching with equal looks of relief and of love. Zack and Jacob move to their sides, and I don't know who to run to first. I feel pulled to all of them, and don't want to choose. Jacob's eye gets my attention, and I walk to him, lifting a hand, placing it on his cheek over the long scar. The scar makes me so angry, knowing the king or his guards must have had something to do with it. Another cost of this war with the king.

"What happened?" I ask carefully, and he leans his head into my hand.

"It's a long story, maybe we should sit as I tell it?" he asks me, and I nod, moving my hand away, but he grabs it and links our fingers.

"Good idea, we have a lot to discuss. Like where exactly you have been for the last year," Ryland says.

"And what exactly the Sea God wants from our little fighter," Zack says with a grin, and the guys all nod. I look around at them, taking in the fact they are all much more muscular than I have ever seen them. They look like they are ready for a fight, and in some ways, it makes it easier to tell them that a fight is what we have coming. If we want a future, we are going to have to fight for it. I keep my thoughts to myself as we all slide into the seats in the small kitchen to sit down. The kitchen is simple, small with wooden cabinets that have seen better days. There's a fireplace for cooking in the corner, with several pans and a kettle resting on it. My eyes instantly go to the boxes and jars of food I can see, knowing that the mountain must have access to a lot of food. The world is starving, but the changed ones are clearly not. I move to sit next to Jacob as he sits down, but he pulls me onto his lap, clearly not willing to part with me, even to just the next seat.

"Why don't you explain what happened when you escaped, and then I will explain what happened with the sea god," I say, wanting my answers first, and Ryland chuckles.

"Still as stubborn as ever, I see," he says, and they all laugh as I roll my eyes at Ryland's reply. He grins at me; the seriousness of his usual expression is nowhere to be seen for a second, until he seems to remember everything we have to overcome.

"Are Everly and Laura here? What about Roger and Tyrion? Even Salty Sam?" I ask, naming them off quickly, and Chaz answers me.

"All safe and alive, don't worry about them for now."

"What about the ship?" I ask.

"Our ship is hidden behind the waterfall with the others." Chaz replies. Relief flitters through me, everyone is safe . . . for now. I have no doubt, it won't be that way for long. War is coming, and the king won't stop until I'm dead. Along with all of my chosen also.

"Why don't I start the story off?" Chaz asks, leaning back in his seat as I look him over, and my eyes lock on his green ones. He looks older, more serious than the last time I saw him. My playful healer, the sweet and kind man I first met is still somewhere deep inside him. Thankfully, he looks better than what he looked like at the castle. I don't think I will ever get the memory of seeing him beat up on that floor, covered in bruises and hanging onto life, out of my head. He never deserved that, not for one second. I try to push the memory of how he looked out of my mind, and focus on his face now, how not one bruise mars it. I nod my head, leaning back against Jacob, who slides an arm around my waist, his thumb rubbing circles on my hip in a soothing motion.

"Once we saw you fall, we knew we had to escape. Hunter and Jacob tried to run into the fire after you, but it exploded. It sent them flying backwards into the cave, which collapsed on top of half of us," I widen my eyes in shock, but Chaz continues with his explanation. "We all wanted to come after you, to save you from the sea, but we couldn't. It wasn't something we could do, even though we desperately wanted to. The cave was blocked, Everly and Laura were stuck under rocks, and most of us were hurt from the collapse," he says.

"We knew you were still alive, our bond told us that much. It's what made it possible for us to pick ourselves up, and get out of the cave," Ryland says.

"I'm so sorry you all had to wait so long for me to come back. I would never have left you intentionally."

"Where were you, Cassandra?" Ryland asks in a lost voice.

"With the sea god; he saved me. For me, it was an hour or less that I was gone, while I was awake anyway," I say, still not believing that the sea god took so much of my life with my chosen away from me. I am thankful he saved me, but he could have warned me that so much time had passed. I watch as my pirates look between each other, none of them look impressed or disbelieving. I know they believe me, without question.

"What else happened when you escaped?" I ask into the silence, and Chaz clears his throat before he starts speaking.

"Everly and Laura weren't harmed too badly when we got them out, and with our help they could stand. Laura is still struggling with the stress and some of her injuries from the collapse, but Everly is fine. We had to carry Jacob and Hunter through the caves, as they were knocked out when they hit the cave. It was difficult, to say the least, until they woke up and could walk for themselves. That's where things really went wrong," Chaz says, drifting off as he looks at Jacob. I look up at him, holding my hand out to his face.

"I'm just so happy you're alive, nothing else matters to me," I whisper to him, but I doubt the others have missed what I said. Jacob's lips turn up in a small smile before he leans down and presses them gently against my forehead. Words aren't needed in this moment, the feelings shown on our faces says it all.

"There were at least thirty guards at the end of

the cave, standing in between us and the ship," Ryland cuts into our moment to explain to me, and then shakes his head.

"It was a bloodbath. Thank the gods that we had weapons on us, but we still had serious injuries . . ." Zack says, looking towards Jacob, and then his eyes drift over to Ryland. Ryland stands up, lifting his white shirt and showing me the five scars littered across his stomach. It's like someone slashed him repeatedly with a sword, over and over again. No one should have been able to survive an attack like that. My heart pounds wildly as Ryland stares at me in silence. I want to go back, make sure none of them are hurt like this. My chosen carry so many scars, scars none of them ever deserved to receive.

"I never believed much in the power of soul mates, of the bond between chosen and changed ones. Well, I didn't until I had five deadly holes in my body that healed themselves, and I lived," Ryland says as he pulls his shirt back down, sitting back in his seat. I turn on Jacob's lap and look up at his eye.

"Then, why didn't this heal? Why are you blind in one eye?" I ask, wanting to fix it, fix him. I can't stand the thought of him in any pain, of being blind in one eye while I'm scar free. He has this because of me.

"Not all things can be fixed, but I survived when it was touch and go for a long time. I have you to thank for that Cass," he says, then kisses my forehead. I almost wish he didn't thank me, but I don't want to take away what he believes.

"Don't thank me. I wasn't there, fighting by your side like I should have been," I say, sliding off of Jacob's lap, and standing up. I look around at them all and down to my hand, where the ring reflects the light in the room. I look back up, my words coming out stronger and more confident than I feel.

"I won't leave your side, never again. I will always be there to protect you from now on. Nothing will separate us, not even the sea god," I declare.

"Not even a god could keep you from us," Ryland says, the challenge in his voice is clear, and I'm glad he feels the same way as I do. That they all feel that way.

"What happened while you were with the sea god?" Hunter asks me, well, more like demands of me.

"I made a deal, an in-depth deal that requires we find a queen, and some other things," I say vaguely.

"Tell us the deal, little fighter," Zack asks.

"A deal is sought after; a deal will be made.

The price is clear, the truth will not be forbidding. The true heir of both water and land must take the throne. The fire-touched king must fall at the hands of the water-touched pirate. Changed ones must never have the throne and only a changed one can give the crown to the new queen. The crown needed to win, can only be found where life lives within water. Only ice will bring the map, if she does not fall. If the deal is not agreed, then the sea will never be saved," I finish off the deal, and they all look between each other.

"Well there is only one person to ask about an heir," Ryland says, and I know he means Laura.

"And the rest?" I ask, because I don't have a clue.

"We will figure it out," Ryland says, and I know a promise when I hear one. A promise from my pirates.

"Can we go and see Everly?" I ask, needing to let her know I'm alive. At the same time, however, I don't want to move from my spot, snuggled in between Chaz and Ryland in front of the stone fireplace in the living room. While Zack has filled me with food, Hunter and Jacob have been explaining the mountains to me. It's difficult to understand it all, but from what I gather, Master Light and four other masters are the leaders of the rebellion here, and they are all changed ones. Ryland reckons there are around three thousand people living in the mountain, but only five hundred of those are changed ones or chosen. Yet everyone supports the changed ones, loves them, and treats them like gods instead of being frightened of them. From what they have told me, there are nothing but good people here, but I want to see that for myself.

"Sure, I will take you to her. She would be training at this time of afternoon," Zack says from where he is leaning against the wall.

"Training?" I ask, curious because the Everly I grew up with never had any interest in fighting or training of any kind.

"Yeah, she trains a lot. We all train . . . but Everly, she never stops. Tyrion stays with her, making sure she actually gets some rest," Zack explains. I slide off the sofa, stretching out as they all watch me. I can see it in the twitch of their fingers, in the way some of them almost get out of their seats, they don't want me to leave. I can't say I want to leave them either, but I need to see Everly is well and alive. She went through so much in the castle, and she is like a sister to me. The only family I have left, really, and I know I won't be able to rest until I see for myself she is good.

"I won't be long," I tell them all gently.

"Go and see your friend. We understand. We know what she means to you," Ryland says firmly. The others don't have to say anything. I can tell they all seem to agree as I look around the room at them. I smile, walking to the door of the little lounge. Zack slides his leather glove-covered hand into my mine as we walk through the kitchen, and down the corridor past the guys' rooms. Zack opens the wooden door for me, leading us outside. It's pretty empty, hardly anyone in sight.

"It's dinner time for most people, so we won't see many others on the way," Zack explains like he can read my thoughts. I rest my head on his arm as we walk down the stone path and up the stairs at the end. The stone is carved so well, with little marks on the higher parts of it. I can't really see what they are, but it looks like dozens of circle marks. I look back up at Zack, wanting to see every little thing that possibly could have changed in the time we were apart. I don't see much difference, though there is more stress, more worry in his kind eyes.

"What has it *really* been like for this last year?" I ask, trusting Zack to tell me everything.

"Knowing you were alive but being unable to find you . . . it was hard. We have all trained and built the army up. Helped out however we could here, just to distract ourselves," he explains to me, and I can picture them all doing just that. It would have been their only way of distracting themselves.

"I wish I could change that, been here for you all," I whisper, but he hears me.

"You are here *now*, that is all that matters in the end," he says, and lifts our hands, kissing the back of my hand gently. I hear the sound of clashing swords in the distance as we get to the end of this pathway and see a huge archway. The archway leads to a massive stone room. It has stone floors, and weapons are littered around the room and are secured on the walls. Right in the middle of the room is Everly, spinning around and smashing her sword into the sword of a guy I don't recognize. Her long hair is up in a bun, her blue eyes seem completely focused as she strikes hit after hit. She has tight black trousers and a white tank top on that make it easier for her to move. All I can think is how much better she looks from the last time I saw her. She's put some weight back on, and maybe even some muscle. I watch her fight the man that is nearly twice her size. Her every hit is precise/perfect, and she seems to know exactly what she is doing. She is so fast as she moves, and I almost don't recognise her as my Everly.

"She is one of the best fighters we have, other than the changed ones. But then, they don't fight fair," Zack whispers to me. We both watch as Everly whacks the other guy, and sends him flying across the room, where he lands outside the rectangle marked on the floor.

"I give up, you win! Everyone is right, you are too good. It's not natural!" the guy huffs, his cheeks bright red. He stands up, storming out of the room past me and Zack.

"Someone's a sore loser," I mutter as I watch the man leave. I can hear Zack's muffled chuckle behind me.

"Cassy?" Everly's shocked voice makes me turn back to her, and she drops her sword on the floor as we stare at each other. We both begin to run towards the other at the same time, crashing together as we meet and embrace each other.

"They were right. You're really alive," she mumbles, pulling back and running her eyes over me.

"I'm back. It's a long story," I explain quickly.

"You're almost glowing, and you look so much better," she says, pulling my arms to her and examining them in clear shock.

"No scars? How?" she asks me.

"Again, a long story, but the short story of it is that it was a gift from the sea god. A gift I didn't ask for," I say, and her eyes widen. "Anyway, how did you learn to fight like that? You look amazing!"

"A lot of training, and I mean a lot. I refuse to be weak ever again, and in case you didn't hear, there's a war coming," she says, walking back over to where she dropped the sword and picking it back up. She puts the sword away and comes back to me, hugging me once more.

"Oh, I know all about the war," I say, stepping away. "I have a lot of things to do and to figure out so we can win this thing, but first, I want to spend the night reconnecting with my *fiancés*," I say, lifting my hand and wiggling my fingers. She stares at my ring as a big grin climbs her face.

"Congratulations, I really mean that. You deserve every happiness, and those pirates are the ones for you," she says and pulls me close. "Your father and mother would have been so proud of you. You marry those pirates and be happy. War or no war, I won't let you lose a chance of your future."

"Thank you, Everly. They are my chosen, and I love them all. I won't let the war stop us being together either," I say simply.

"From what I've learnt of chosen and changed ones here, they are your soulmates, and nothing can stop souls who are destined for each other from being together," she says, and hugs me once more before stepping back.

"Go before I hug you again and have a good night. Can you come and see me tomorrow? I want to catch up, and I have some things to tell you," she asks me.

"Like what?" I ask curiously, and she looks behind me to Zack at the door giving us some privacy.

"Things we need to be *alone* to discuss," she says quietly.

"Sure, I will see you tomorrow then," I place my hand on her shoulder and gently squeeze. "I'm so happy you are alive and well," I say, and she nods with a small grin.

"I'm more than well. I'm finally home," she says with a small smile on her lips I watch her go as she walks away. Zack comes to my side, sliding an arm around my shoulders.

"Let's go back to our home," Zack whispers close to my ear. Instantly, I relax as he speaks of home. That's exactly where I want to be.

"Our home is on a ship, but for now, this will do," I mumble.

"Your home is with your pirates, no matter where we are, on land or at sea," he says, kissing the side of my head, and making me smile.

"That's true," I sigh.

"Is that what you see for our future? All of us on our ship together?" he asks me, and I rest my head against his chest, sliding my arm around his back as we walk out of the room.

"It's my dream. I want us to be free, and together. I can see us all on our ship, rescuing changed ones, and bringing them here with their chosen and families. Helping people and travelling the world. I spent so much of my childhood and teenage years stuck on one island and hating it. I know it was necessary, but if we are going to fight for freedom, I want to truly be free," I explain to him.

"I want that for you. I want to show you everything in Calais. You have seen so much of a world full of horrors, but little of its true beauty that is underneath the surface," Zack says as we walk down the stone steps. Both of us go silent as two people in hoods walk past us. I'm only able to catch a glimpse of purple hair and purple eyes that almost seem to glow as we pass them. I turn back as we get to the bottom of the steps and see the man is looking back at me, but he turns away before I can make out anything else about him.

"I don't want to talk about that place, so tell me something else. Anything else," I implore as I face back forward, knowing I'm not ready to face the memories of my time with the king. I may have survived, and I may not have any scars on the outside, but there are plenty on the inside. I know I have to deal with them at some point, but it will have to be sometime in the future. Hopefully in the future when there isn't a war, and I know I'm safe. I'm not safe here, and that's the problem. It's all an illusion, because the king will never let me be free. One of us has to die, I'm determined that it's not going to be me.

"You don't have to put on a brave face for me, little fighter," he says and stops as we get to our door, holding it open for me.

"It's not a brave face, Zack. It's just I don't want to spend too much more time focusing on the past and not the future," I say, leaning up and kissing his rough-feeling cheek.

"So where should I sleep?" I ask awkwardly as Zack shuts the door behind us. He smiles, holding out a hand for me. I slide my hand into his without a second thought, and he leads me to the first door on the left. He opens it, and we walk into the bedroom hand in hand. It's a big room, with a large bed with blue sheets and two candles lit on the bedside cabinets.

"We left this room for you," he says, "I'll leave you to get some sleep . . ."

"Don't," I say with a bit of panic. "Can't you stay with me? I don't want to be away from you," I ask, grabbing his arm, and he turns slightly. His eyes lock with mine, and neither of us wants to look away as I await his decision. He doesn't answer, but goes to the door and shuts it, staying in the room with me.

"Cassandra, you deserve so much more than me . . .," he begins as he walks towards me, sliding his leather-gloved hands onto my face, "but if you will have me, I'm yours. I will never leave your side, and I will always love you." He kisses me before I can say a word, a harsh, but beautiful, kiss that takes my breath away. He pulls back, making sure my eyes are locked with his as he speaks.

"I'm not pretty, not under all this," he says, and I shake my head.

"I love you for you, and for every scar you have, because it shows your bravery. I love every mark on your skin because it shows you're a survivor. They make you who you are, Zack, and they are beautiful," I say, and pull his hands from my face. He doesn't move as I pull each of his gloves off, pausing to kiss each hand before letting them go.

"Cassandra," he warns as I start unbuttoning his shirt. I don't stop, even though his gravelly voice makes my hands shake a little, and sends goose bumps all over my skin. I pull his shirt over his shoulder, before smoothing my hands over his chest and feeling all the little scars that are littered around. I lean down, kissing each one, falling to my knees as I work my way down, and then I reach for his belt. I look up, locking my eyes with his as I undo his belt, and his trousers fall to his ankles. I take his length into my hand at first, before leaning forward and sucking the tip into my mouth, swirling my tongue around it as he moans. I've never done this, and I have no idea what I'm doing, but the noises he is making suggests I'm doing something right. Inch by inch I attempt to take him deeper into my mouth, but he slides his hands into my hair and gently pulls me up.

"I've never done this, you're my first, and if you keep doing that, it's going to be over far too quickly. I want to see you first," he explains to me and slams his lips onto mine. I wrap my legs around him as he walks us to the bed, his length pressed against me, but my dress stops us. He lays me on the bed and leans over, using his hands to slowly pull my dress off me until I'm naked in front of him.

"I dreamed about you, about seeing you like this," he says, running a hand from my neck down to my breast, making me gasp when his rough hand slides over my nipple. "But dreams are nothing like the real thing, not one tiny bit," he says as he reaches my core and rubs a finger over my swollen nub.

"Zack," I gasp, and he rubs faster, making me feel so close to the edge that it's borderline painful. Just when I think I'm going to come, he suddenly stops. He grabs my hips and rolls me on top of him, his length easily sliding straight into me. I moan, losing all control as I start riding him and feel his hands dig into my hips as his head arches back. I come harder than I ever have before, screaming out his name. Zack finishes with me, and I collapse onto his chest, both of us breathing heavily. We are silent for a long time, with him still inside me until he finally pulls out, but still keeps me close.

"Zack?" I ask.

"Yes?" he replies.

"Want to do that again?" I inquire, and I feel him harden against my leg. He grins down at me before rolling me over. He slips back into me once more, making me moan out loud.

"Little fighter, I'm definitely not done with you yet," he says and kisses me thoroughly.

Chapter Three

Cassandra

"Little fighter," Zack whispers in my ear, making me blink open my groggy eyes. I see him lifted up on his elbow, with his golden hair falling into his eyes as he looks down at me. I find myself staring at my mark on his forehead for a while. It's strange how quickly I've grown used to seeing my mark on all my pirates. It's so normal.

"Morning," I say, even though we haven't been sleeping long, yet I don't regret *not* sleeping one little bit. I trace my hand over his chest, and he closes his eyes with a contented hum before grabbing my hand and pulling it to his lips.

"Thank you for last night . . . I never expected it to be that amazing," he admits.

"I never expected me to be your first. I remember you saying you had a girlfriend once . . . and I assumed," I say, blushing a little.

"We were too young for that. We only ever had a few stolen kisses," he says.

"What was her name?" I ask, mildly jealous of his first kiss. At the same time, I know he lost her, and it made him who he is today. I have her to thank for who my Zack is; she helped him get to where he is.

"Kasa," he says, kissing my forehead. There are a few knocks on the door before it abruptly bangs open.

"Morning, you both look . . . refreshed," Dante teases. Chaz walks in after him, rolling his eyes as I sit up and attempt to keep the blanket wrapped around myself. Zack doesn't care about nudity it seems, as he gets out of bed and starts pulling his trousers on.

"We didn't mean to interrupt, but there is a meeting for Cassandra in an hour," Chaz explains.

"And I'm hungry," Dante shrugs, giving Zack a pointed look.

"Fine, I will make something for you to hopefully choke on," Zack says playfully as he grabs his shirt and walks towards the door. "Toasted banana sand-wiches?" Zack turns to ask me, and I nod with a small grin that matches his. I couldn't think of a better food to eat right now. Zack and Dante walk out, leaving me alone with Chaz.

"There are clothes in the drawers that are yours, I think I got your size right. And the shower room is through there," he says, almost awkwardly. I stand up, with the blanket still wrapped around me and walk over to him.

"Is everything okay?" I ask, and he sighs quietly, reaching forward and pushing a little bit of my hair behind my ear.

"I'm worried. The masters . . . I don't know what they are going to say or what they are going to ask from you. I'm worried about you," he says in a soft voice.

"Don't be worried, no one is ever going to control me. No one." I say firmly, and he smiles widely.

"I forgot how strong you are, how inspiring," he comments, stroking his fingers down my cheek, "and how utterly stunning." I lean closer and press a light kiss to his lips, before moving back.

"Thank you," I say, feeling a little overwhelmed, but in the best way. I feel lucky, so lucky, I have all these amazing pirates in my life. It's almost funny to think back to the times I used to be scared of pirates and fearful of the sea. Both the sea and my pirates are now *everything* to me.

"Get dressed and ready. The masters are a fearful bunch of changed ones, though all extremely powerful and smart. You have to remember they have never had a woman changed one around. They might be stuck in their ways and not want anything to do with you," he warns me.

"I will be careful, but they *will* listen to me. I will have you all at my sides anyway, right?" I ask, but Chaz shakes his head with an annoyed look.

"No, chosen aren't allowed in the masters' rooms, only changed ones. It's a magically blessed room, blessed by the sea god. It literally stops us, or anyone who isn't a changed one, from walking in," he explains to me.

"Will you be outside at least?" I ask.

"Always," he kisses my cheek and walks out of the room, shutting the door behind him. I drop the blanket, not needing it anymore since I'm alone, and go to the other door in the room. It's another cave room, but the walls are smoothed down, and a string hangs from the ceiling near the door. Natural light shines in the room from a small hole in the wall, but it's still a little dark. I pull the string, and water comes out of the wall like a waterfall, splashing onto the floor and draining into the hole in the corner. I step in, moaning at the feel of the warm water. It's not very warm, but it's not cold, and that's a bonus. I wash my hair with the soap I find, putting it back and looking up at the water. I know I can't control my powers, not really, but I want to learn. It has to be possible to learn somehow. I reach into myself, feeling for the bond to my pirates, and then trying to control the water. I stare for ages, but nothing happens, and I drop my hand, feeling a little disappointed. My powers come out when I'm scared, but it's too powerful, too much water releases, and it takes over me. I don't like that, I want to have some control over my power. I get out of the shower, stepping onto the cold stone and grabbing a towel off a stone shelf I see in the corner. I dry my hair before wrapping the towel around myself and walking back into my still empty room.

"Time is drawing near, you must speak to her, and then leave the mountains, my changed one," the sea god's voice whispers in my mind, powerful enough to nearly make me fall to me knees. I lean against the

wall, holding my hand to my head as he speaks one more time.

"Time is not on your side; the deal must be accomplished . . . or you will pay the price." His voice finally disappears from my head, leaving me with a headache and a deep worry about the threat at the end of that. *What price?*

Chapter Four

Cassandra

Tucking my blue shirt into my high trousers, I look down and examine the rest of my outfit. I have on knee-high leather boots and leather cuffs that match on my wrists. I brush my long hair and pull it up into a high ponytail in the mirror, before stepping back. I look so different, it's like everything has changed, other than my mark. I'm older, hopefully smarter, and more loved than I've ever been. I know I need to finish this war and end the king's life. He took my father, Miss Drone, and Livvy from me. Even if Livvy betrayed me in the end, she was still only a young, foolish girl stuck in a horrible situation. I steel my back, look at the hazel eyes of my reflection, and nod to myself before turning and walking out of my bedroom. As I walk down the corridor towards the kitchen, only the sound of my boots clicking against the stone and the distant noise of voices can be heard.

"Little bird, you look every bit the fiancé of six pirates," Hunter's gravelly voice says, and I turn to see him just behind me, leaning against the door frame of one of the other rooms. His black shirt is unbuttoned, highlighting his chiselled chest and putting his delectable abs on display. I trail my eyes over him, all the way down to his black trousers and heavy looking leather boots. When I look back up, his dark hair is slightly wavy with his purple feather tied into the ends of one of the many braids woven into his hair. I can see my mark on his forehead, it suits him. I finally glance down, to see the amused smirk on his lips, his deep blue eyes burning with a darkness I want to fall into. I've read somewhere that most people are scared of the darkness, and that they prefer the light. Yet, I like the darkness because it's quiet, safe, and so very seductive.

"When will I be the wife of six pirates?" I ask him, loving the sound of his seductive chuckle as he walks over to me.

"Impatient?" he asks, the word pronounced slowly, giving me time to stare into his eyes as he pulls me to him.

"Always, *pirate*," I say, and he grins before kissing me deeply.

"We have ten minutes until we have to leave, and Cass hasn't eaten yet," Jacob says, and I pull away from the kiss, ignoring the annoyed look that crosses Hunter's face.

"Coming," I say, turning and walking over to Jacob who waits by the door. He holds it open, letting me into the kitchen where Ryland is sitting down at the table with Zack, but he doesn't follow me in. Ryland looks more like his brother now, maybe because he doesn't have on his pirate hat or the cloth he used to wear around his neck. Ryland's hair is braided in places, and the top half is pulled away from his face. His blue eyes meet mine, and I realise he has his father's eyes, more so than his mother's. They are lighter almost, but I'm not scared of them when Ryland stares at me. He looks at me like he would jump in front of an army for me.

"Where are Chaz and Dante? And where has Jacob gone?" I ask, as I sit down next to Ryland and clear my thoughts as I look between him, Zack, and Hunter. I smile when I look down at the toasted banana sandwich waiting for me and the glass of water.

"We all have duties here for our jobs and to earn

our food. Everyone is given a job in the mountain to make sure it runs well," Ryland explains to me.

"What kind of jobs?" I ask, and take a bite of the sandwich, chewing it slowly as Ryland explains.

"Washing, cooking, helping the changed ones with the plants, getting water, feeding the dragons, cleaning the ships, and the one we all regularly do, training the army," he lists them for me.

"It makes sense, and it's amazing to hear that everyone works together here, with the changed ones and not against them," I comment before finishing off my sandwich. Picking up the water off the table, I down the rest of it.

"It is amazing here. Everyone has a common goal and fear," Zack says as he picks up some of the plates and takes them to the sink.

"Or some may say a common hate," Hunter interjects with a note of sarcasm.

"Everyone here hates the king and wants him dead?" I guess.

"Correct," Ryland replies with no emotion evident in his tone. You wouldn't know we were talking about the death of his father, not with how he says it. Ryland must see something in my reaction because he tilts his head to the side.

"He is not, and never really was, any kind of

father to me. Any bond that we may have had because of blood was lost the moment he laid a hand on you," he tells me firmly.

"And no one gets away with hurting you, Cassandra," Hunter tells me, and I stand up, pushing my chair in.

"Then it's time I hear whatever plan you've got. We need to get on with what we have to do here before we take this army to the king, and I kill him," I say.

"You won't be killing him. He isn't going anywhere near you ever again," Hunter demands gruffly.

"It has to be me, and you have to support me on this, or it will never work. It's in the deal I made with the Sea God. He must die at my hand, and I'm the only one strong enough to stand a chance against him anyway," I say, not waiting for a response from any of them. Walking out of the room, I hear multiple footsteps behind me. I turn as I open the main door, and see all of their expressions as they follow after me. Hunter doesn't appear impressed. In fact, he looks seconds away from throwing me over his shoulder and carrying me off somewhere where I can't get myself hurt. Ryland has a look of both amusement and worry, which actually also matches Zack's expression quite well.

"This goes against everything in us, but if we know anything about you, Cassandra, it's that we won't be able to stop you, only support you. Don't think you are doing this alone, though." Ryland says, and I nod at him.

"I want to support you more than anything, but I'm just frightened of you being up against the king once again," Zack says, and I understand his fear.

"I'm not the girl I was when I first got to that castle, and I will not stop until the king is dead. The world needs him dead, and I can't live in a world where he continues to breathe. You're right, the price of what I want is high. It's risky, but it needs to be done, and I need you all at my side to do it," I say, pausing to wait for their reply.

"You will always have me at your side little bird, but I won't let you die," Hunter tells me and walks out the door. Zack simply kisses my cheek as he passes me, and I know he doesn't need to say it. He feels the same as Hunter does. I walk out the door, the light from the gap in the middle of the mountain momentarily blinding me. There are people everywhere, walking past us and continuing down the stairs as they go about their normal day. The people here are all so diverse; they appear to be from different islands and of all skin colours. Yet, they are all here, coexisting together. I walk past them, only catching glimpses of their faces as they stare at me. Most don't look as they rush around the steps, carrying woven string bags and books in their arms.

"You're her! The one that fought the king and survived! The princess changed one!" a random girl shouts with an excited squeal, running over with three of her friends at her side. They all seem to be around ten years old, with excited smiles as they wait for me to say anything. *What do I say?*

"Yes, I did, but I'm not a princess," I answer, and the girl jumps up and down.

"And you came to win the war, so my brother can be free! So all the changed ones can be, and you can rule as the new queen! I want to be just like you when I'm older!" she exclaims, and a young man runs over to us. His long black hair is pulled back, so I can see his changed mark on his forehead. It's heart shaped, with half of it filled in. It suits the shade of his dark brown eyes and hair.

"I'm so sorry for the children," he bows at me. I go to say something when he says to the children, "Girls we have school to attend, and you know you can't be late," he says, clapping his hands, and they all run off giggling.

"It was nice to meet them. Hello, I'm Cassandra," I say, holding out my hand, and he shakes it. His eyes glow a yellow colour, and he lets go suddenly.

"Take care, Cassandra, maybe we can speak again sometime soon. My name is Ace," he says with a nod, and then runs off before I can even agree.

"What do you think his gift is?" I ask Ryland as he steps to my side, and Hunter goes to the other.

"No idea, but I would guess an element power. From what I've seen of changed ones' power, most seem to stem from the ground, from the very roots of Calais. Like your water," Ryland answers.

"I can't wait to see another changed one use their gifts. It will be so odd for me," I say, and Ryland slides an arm around my waist. Zack stays behind us as we walk through the people on the stairs. We walk around and around the caves, going up five flights of stairs. Once we reach the top, we walk around to a bridge that passes over the waterfall. This is the very top of the mountain by the looks of it. The top of the waterfall is visible, with a cave just above it. The bridge is made out of stone and covered in little drawings. There are two large dragon statues that hold a rose flower in between them. The stone rose looks like it has blood dripping down it for a second, but when I look away and back again, it's just stone.

"Blood for the crown, time is short," the sea god whispers suddenly, the power of his voice making me sway a little, and Ryland holds me to him. Hunter and Zack step closer as I hold my hands to my head. Just as abruptly as he appeared, the sea god is gone, leaving me with another headache. *Why do I feel like the sea god is getting more and more desperate?*

"What was that? Your eyes and mark were glowing a blue colour," Hunter asks me, rubbing a finger over my mark. Zack rubs a hand down my arm soothingly, as I try to get my words out.

"The sea god, still whispering but it's different than it was in the dungeons. It's almost frantic, demanding," I tell them, and look back up at the rose. *Blood for the crown, but whose blood?*

"I have to meet the masters. This can't stop me from doing that. He can't stop me," I say, but I know the sea god didn't really want to stop me. Maybe he was trying to warn me of something, but I have no idea what. I step away from my pirates, who don't look pleased but let me go.

"We can't go any further," Ryland says just as I'm about to step onto the bridge. I feel it suddenly as

I stand under the statue of the dragons and the rose. There's a power coming from the bridge, and when I concentrate, I can see that the bridge is faintly glowing a blue colour now. I look back at my pirates, the three of them standing watching and supporting me even if they can't follow me here. I know if I was in danger, they would find a way to bring the mountain down to make sure I was safe. Their love gives me strength to hold my head high, knowing that the next things I do will be so important to our future.

"Be safe, but we trust you," Zack says, placing a hand on Ryland and Hunter's shoulders as he stands in the middle of them.

"I will be back soon," I tell them firmly, and lift my head, as I turn and walk across the bridge.

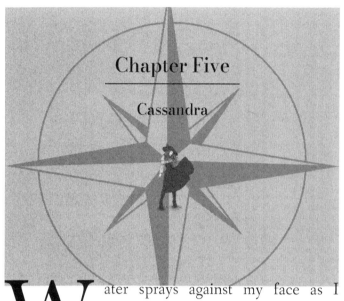

Chapter Five

Cassandra

Water sprays against my face as I slowly walk over the bridge, to the open cave entrance on the other side that comes into view. The bridge is covered all the way down, with carvings of dragons and of a man controlling water. The sea god is depicted as well. There are words I can't read inscribed all the way down it. I wonder what they say, what they speak of, and if it's of any use for me to understand the sea god. I stop near the edge of the bridge, tracing my finger over the upside-down triangle I spot carved on the banister of the bridge. It looks just like my mark. I wonder if another changed one has had my mark before, if maybe the mark is reborn time and time again.

"Cassandra of Onaya. The first female changed one to live in many, many years. It is an honour to meet you," a man says from the shadow of the cave. The man steps forward into the dim light, his face hidden under a cloak. He lowers the hood as I step off the bridge, and move to stand right in front of him. It is the master I met when I landed here yesterday, the one that advised me. Dante seemed to trust him. I run my eyes over his fragile form and realise he is a lot older than I first thought he was. His white hair matches his pale eyes. I find myself focusing my eyes on his changed mark, still finding it strange to see other changed ones. I doubt I will ever be able to get used to it.

"Master Light, there is another female changed one who lives. She is queen and should be respected. It is not her fault what happened to her, and she is one of our kind. We must not forget her. I will not," I say, hating that she is overlooked like this. She may not have her senses, and she may have lost her mind, but she should be remembered. She is queen after all, and that demands respect on its own.

"You are correct, of course," he says, but his tone doesn't suggest he cares much for my opinion of the queen. I doubt anyone will care much for her anymore, but she is Hunter and Ryland's mother. I feel nothing but a deep sorrow for her and hope I can save her somehow. "Come inside, we have much to discuss." I follow him into the cave, which opens up into a massive room. There is a table made out of solid white crystal in the centre of the cavern. There are four other figures wearing hoods sitting at the table, and Master Light walks ahead, holding out the seat at the top of the table for me.

"Please sit, Cassandra," he asks me. I take a seat where he indicates as he sits on the other side of the table. I smooth my hands over the stone, feeling the circle patterns etched into it. It is utterly beautiful and precious. I don't think I've ever seen a piece of crystal this big before.

"I am Master Light, as you well know," he introduces himself again, "please introduce yourselves, masters." They all take their hoods down at the same time, and I look at the masters on my right first. One is the purple-haired man I encountered last night. He nods respectfully, which is much different from the look I received when I saw him last. I don't know why, but I instantly don't trust this master. There is something about him, and I will be watching my back around him.

"My name is Master Igor," he says bluntly, quickly turning away and not waiting for any reaction from me. I look over to the man on his other side, who appears so much different. This man has five large cuts over his face, almost covering up his mark but I can still see it. It's a circle, with some swirls inside. His grey eyes watch me with a lot of intelligence hiding behind them.

"Master Hid, at your service," he says, bowing his head.

"There is no need to bow to me," I say, and he chuckles.

"Your chosen are the princes of Calais, that makes you a princess by all accounts. If that didn't garner my respect, what I have heard you did with the king earns you my respect for the rest of your life. Respect is earnt in actions, and you have done just that. A girl from Onaya, with nothing more than a mark, nearly killed the king and then vowed to go back. Most people would be scared, scarred, and destroyed from what I heard happened. But you are strong, resilient, and so very impressive, Cassandra of Onaya," he says, and I stay silent, not knowing how to respond to that statement. Anything I did was to survive, until the king took everything he could from me and promised to take more, to destroy my world. I won't let anyone take my chosen from me, and fighting back is the only way I know I will be able to survive this. I thought I did what anyone else would do, but maybe Master Hid is right.

"You also have my respect, Cassandra. I am Master Pirate," I turn at the sound of a deep voice to see the man who spoke on my left. He is a huge man, with an arrow mark on his forehead, wavy hair that falls around his face, and a serious expression.

"Pirate?" I ask.

"My family name. My ancestors were some of the very first pirates, and I have forty ships that my family run. I left the king after he decided killing my child was the best way to control me. I want revenge for my little boy, and my army of ships will bring an army to his door and help me do just that," he explains to me.

"I am sorry the king took your son's life. He seems to think killing is the way to control everyone, and it is not. He will pay for every life stolen, I swear," I say firmly. Master Pirate nods, his eyes on me like he is looking into my soul to determine if I'm telling the truth. When he finds whatever he is looking for, he smiles slowly.

"I believe the king should have killed you when he had the chance, because he has clearly created his greatest enemy," Master Pirate says, and I smirk. I look up at his mark, curious what the arrow means, what his power is.

"What is your gift?" I ask.

"We don't know this girl, just heard rumours, and we are to trust her with everything? All of our secrets? She could be working with the king, or the princes–her lovers–could be!" the final master shouts, slamming his pale hand on the table. I lock eyes with green ones that match the green plant-shaped mark on his forehead. He seems to be about my age, with blonde hair, a body built from rigorous training, and an outraged expression. I'm sure he doesn't trust anyone, and I imagine he has lost much to make him this way.

"If we as changed ones don't trust each other, who can we trust?" I ask, and he tilts his head to the side.

"We are meant to trust each other simply because a god kissed us at birth, cursing us? Because we have all been cursed to be hunted? To have those we loved hunted? To know we are never safe?" he rapidly questions me, his angry eyes never leaving mine.

"You believe your mark to be a curse?" I ask quietly. I understand the sentiment, it is something I used to believe when I was on Onaya. I thought it was a curse because of what our ancestors did, because it kept me locked in the house, hidden away. The mark is not a curse, I know that now. It's a gift, a gift that gives as much as it takes.

"Everyone I have ever loved is dead because of this mark, what else would you call it?" he snaps.

"That's enough Master Gold," Master Light says, and I raise my hand.

"He is right to speak what he feels. There is no point to this meeting if we all lie to each other. We are trying to make a new world, and it shouldn't be started with lies," I respond. Master Light raises his eyebrows at me with an impressed expression, and I turn to look at the other masters.

"I once believed my mark to be a curse, but only because this world and the king makes it so. Yet, we have power. We are blessed by a god, and we can make the world a better place. You can trust me because we have a common goal that everyone on this mountain shares," I say, and Master Gold doesn't say anything, letting me speak. "We all want the king dead, for the changed ones to be free, and to change this world for the better. I will fight for that with or without your help, but your help could be the difference between victory and defeat."

"You speak a good bargain, yet, share no plan on

how to win," Master Gold replies, neither agreeing nor disagreeing with me.

"I made a deal with the sea god, and the deal tells us all we need to know to win this war," I say, and they are all silent.

"Tell us the deal," Master Light finally responds, and I recite it for them. They all look around at each other, and Master Pirate quickly writes down my words on a notepad.

"You have met the sea god?" Master Light is again the first to ask after another long silence.

"Yes, he saved me when I fell off a cliff at the king's palace. He looked after me, spoke to me about things. I was offered more than one deal, but that is the deal I accepted," I say.

"He saved you when you fell into the sea?" Master Pirate questions me.

"Yes," I reply simply. "The sea god needs me alive to win this for him, and he is always watching us, always wanting his children to survive."

"None of us will survive while the king lives."

"The sea god created the monster of the king we have. It was an accident, I believe. He never meant to make the king the bitter monster he is now. Even gods make mistakes, and their children must be the ones to fix it," I tell them, and there's an eerie silence to the room as they take in my words.

"Then this deal, how can it help us figure out our next move?" Master Hid asks.

"We need a crown, a god-blessed crown that is the twin of the one the king wears. It boosts powers, and that is what makes the king so very formidable. It is what enabled him to steal the gifts from his changed one, the queen. The king stole both crowns from the sea god, and I believe the deal tells us he hid it with the mermaids," I say, knowing deep down I'm right. 'Where life lives in the sea,' can only be the mermaids, who are more likely to kill us than help us.

"So, we get this crown, and then you will kill him as we use our army to destroy his?" Master Light muses. "It could work, but we will need time to prepare."

"That's the plan, but I need to find the crown first. The king hid it with the mermaids for a reason. They won't just give it to us, and I know nothing of mermaids, or how to fight them," I reply.

"You're missing an important part of all of this. The king cannot die while his changed one lives. To win this war, you must kill the queen. If you promise us that, we will give you use of our army. We will let you lead, as well as help you find the crown and what to do to bargain with the mermaids. Mermaids like deals, treaties, and most importantly, tricks," Master Light informs me in a serious tone.

"She will be my mother in law . . . she doesn't deserve to die. The king destroyed every part of her and stole her power. Death is not what should befall her," I plead with them, despite knowing nothing will change their minds or save the queen. Her death is needed, and I know that, I just don't want to accept it.

"Her mind is lost. Her other chosen were burnt away into nothing, nothing left but dust and not even changed magic can heal that. She would welcome death," Master Hid tells me with a touch of under-standing in his voice.

"But changed ones' chosen cannot die? So, how did they? I don't understand, though I never really thought about it until now," I ask them all quietly.

"The only known way to kill chosen when their changed one still lives is to burn their body. How can anyone come back from that?" Master Pirate muses, and leans back in his seat. "But perhaps the souls are more important than the bodies we wear. Soul mates speak nothing of our bodies, only our souls." I think about what he says as they all watch me closely.

Everyone in this room believes in so much more than life and death.

"Do we have a deal, Cassandra? Will you kill the queen?" Master Light asks me. The question in itself is simple, but it breaks my heart when I try to answer it. Even in my mind, I cannot say the words, let alone speak them out loud. Is one life worth giving the whole world a chance? Especially, when that life is an innocent one?

"Why me?" I blurt out.

"Because it proves you will give *everything* up to win this war. Even the respect and love of two of your chosen. Even your soul for killing an innocent," Master Light says, his tone gentle but firm. He wants an answer, and I keep my eyes on the table as I think it through. I know she has to die, but I don't honestly know if I could be the one to kill her. She is Hunter and Ryland's mother, and they love her. They would hate me for killing her. Despite all that, in the end I know my answer. There has only ever been one possible answer.

"I will kill her," I whisper, hating myself for saying it, but knowing I don't have a choice. *If my soul and my chosen, are the price for saving the world, how can I be selfish enough not to pay it?*

Chapter Six

Cassandra

"Spend the day looking around and finding your place here, but we expect you at training when you are called," Master Light says as I step out of the room, and he walks with me.

"Training?" I ask, curious.

"Of your powers. Master Gold will be training you, as he is best at pushing one's skills to the furthest they can be stretched. The crown will boost your powers, but they are no use if you have no control. You are more likely to sink an island into the sea, than save anyone," he explains, and I nod, knowing he has a point. I've never had any control over my powers. They just attack when they are needed. "On every fifth evening, you will attend the master's meetings . . . Master Cassandra."

"I'm a master now?" I ask, not sure if I even I want to be one. I'm not sure how long I can spend here, because I have to leave to get the crown. I can't risk the king going to get the crown before me, and destroying it.

"You are a master, a princess, and our leader," he says, shocking me.

"Titles mean nothing if you do not earn them, and I have not," I tell him.

"But you will, and that is all that matters here, Cassandra. The sea god chose you to lead us to the light, to peace, and to a new world." I don't have a response for him, letting his words fill my mind as if the sea god just said them himself. I go to walk away, as I need to think, but his words stop me. "Spend this time with your pirates, because the war will have a price, and perfect, happy memories are priceless."

"How do you know there will be a price?" I ask him.

"There is always a price to stop darkness and gain peace. If it was easy, it would have been done already. We wouldn't have waited for you," he says and turns around, walking away from me. There won't be any price, not for my pirates. I refuse to let that happen. I turn and walk over the bridge, enjoying the water splashing against me, and letting it soothe me in a way. Hunter and Ryland are leaning against the bridge entrance. Both of their heads snap up when they see me. The brothers stand tall as they watch me walk to them, their eyes blazing with desire and relief that I'm back. I can almost feel it in our bond, like a wave of emotion coming from them. *I wonder if they can feel what I feel? Is the bond one-sided?*

"Where is Zack?" I ask when I get to them, and Hunter puts an arm around my shoulder, pulling me to his side.

"Someone has come to the mountains on ships with the people of Sixa, and they claim to know Zack. They asked to see you, demanded actually. Zack went ahead with Jacob to see if they are safe," he explains. I know Zack would never let anyone near me that he didn't trust.

"From his home?" I ask, wondering who it could be. He never told me much of his home, but I remember him saying there was a friend called Shan. A friend he grew up with. Maybe that's who it is. *But why would they need to see me?*

"Yes, all the people of Sixa have apparently left their homes, and come to join the war," Hunter continues, walking over to the side of the cave, and I follow him over. Looking down the mountain, I see a huge group of people in big fur coats, with massive white tigers next to them. There must be over a thousand people standing there, but I can't see much more about them.

"They have disobeyed the king and sided with the mountains. With you," Ryland says as he steps next to me.

"Wow . . . why?" I ask, but Ryland isn't the one that answers me. A female does in a demanding voice, and I turn to face her.

"Because, changed one, we believe you can finish him. You can win a war, but you will need my help," the woman states, standing about ten feet away from me. She is stunning, with long black hair and a long white fur cloak covering her body. Zack walks at her side, with Jacob on the other, and four massive guys follow behind her. They look like a wall of muscle, and the protective way they stand guard over the woman lets me know she is someone important to them.

"Who are you?" I ask, and Zack walks over, holding my hand.

"This is Wynn, and these are her husbands. They saved me once, and I consider them friends," he explains to me and turns to Wynn. "This is my fiancé, Cassandra." Her whole face lights up in a big smile, and it makes me smile, too. She is clearly happy that Zack is settled.

"Congratulations, Zack, you lucky bastard," the big guy says, walking over and patting Zack's shoulder as Zack lightly laughs. The man turns to me, holding out a hand.

"My name is Shan. I hope you love my friend, or I'm going to find out if chucking a changed one into the sea will actually kill them," he says in a friendly manner, and I laugh, ignore his protective threat, and shake his huge hand.

"I can tell you it wouldn't work," I chuckle letting go of his hand. Ryland moves behind me, wrapping his hands around my waist possessively, and resting his chin on my head.

"And *I* can tell you that you wouldn't make it within two inches of our Cassandra. She would kill you before we could even get to you," Ryland says, and both of them stare each other down until Wynn slides in between Shan and me.

"Boys, stop with the manly bullshit. We have other, more important things to discuss," Wynn snaps, and grins up at Shan when he wraps his arm around her waist. They look at each other like there is no one else in the world, and it makes me smile. This is what life is about, these simple moments of love. These moments of something pure.

"We need to show her," one of the other men says, carrying an old-looking box over to us. The other two men talk quietly with each other, before coming over. We all hear a loud roar, followed by a few bangs. I look over at Hunter, who is looking over the cliff.

"Seems your people have started a fight. You might want to look into that," he darkly chuckles, and there's another loud roar from the crowd below.

"Someone needs to check on the people, so we will go be with them," one of Wynn's men says with a slightly worried look that he shares with his friend. Wynn kisses them both before they leave.

"I'm Fen, nice to meet you all," the man that stayed behind says, and hands Wynn the box as she comes back to us. She walks over to me, holding the box out in front of her.

"Open it," she says, and I look over at Zack, who nods. He clearly trusts her. I smile at him, before lifting the box open and seeing the old map inside. I lift it out, and stretch it wide. It's a map of Calais, and it's extremely detailed and very old.

"I can't read a map like this, so what are we looking at?" I ask, and Ryland steps over to me.

"Why don't you let the pirates have a look at the map? It's kinda what we are good at," he says, but it's playful and makes me laugh.

"No, you can look and then explain to me," I exclaim, and he chuckles kissing my lips softly.

"And you say I'm stubborn."

"You are," I laugh. I look around, spotting the rocks on the floor, and walking over to them. I kneel down, placing the rocks on the corners of the map gently.

"It's a map, and it leads to the only place I don't want to ever return," Hunter says, leaning over, and Ryland examines the map on my other side. He takes my hand pointing to the three circles that are engraved in the Lost Sea, just below Thron.

"That is where the mermaids live. Their castles are below the sea," Ryland states. There's silence between all of us as I stand up and look at Wynn.

"What is located there?" I ask, but I know the answer. This looks like a map to the crown, to the only place it could be, but how did a girl from Sixa get it?

"The lost crown, the one the king hid. This was also in the box," she pulls out a long purple stone, shaped almost like a stick. There's a power to it, I can feel it from here.

"And what is that, exactly?" I ask.

"I don't know, but the mermaids will want something in exchange for the crown . . . I believe they will trade for this," she says, walking over. Wynn hands it to me, but holds her hand over mine on the stick. Her eyes lock with mine, and I see enough emotion to not want to move.

"My mother died, and her last request of me was to get this box to you. We all believe in you, and when we go to war, I *will* fight at your side. Keep this safe, please," she says in an emotion-filled voice. I know from the look in her eyes she means every single word, and I give her a sharp nod. I will keep this safe for her and for everyone else. Let's pray the mermaids want the stick badly enough to give up the crown. She doesn't say anything more, just walks away with her husbands following her. I look down at the stick in my hand. It doesn't look like much, but it could be everything to the mermaids.

"The deal I made said we had to find the crown where life lives in the sea. I guess we know where we need to go, and now we have something to actually give them," I muse.

"But, can we go? The mountain needs us, and the army isn't ready yet," Ryland asks.

"I need to speak to the masters, and devise a plan. If we can plan it right, so we would be on our way back from the mermaids as they took their army across the seas . . . it could work," I say, thinking over the plan I will have to give them. The army will need to go around the Storm Sea, so we will have a few weeks I think.

"Master Cassandra, your dragon is causing a big fuss outside. We need you to come and calm her." Master Pirate says, coming over the bridge and catching a glimpse of the map on the floor before Hunter picks it up. I hand the stick to Ryland behind my back, trusting him to hide it. It's not that I don't trust Master Pirate. I've just learnt not to trust strangers, and I'm not stupid enough to tell him everything.

"Let's go then, I don't know the way to my dragon. Would you show me, Master Pirate?" I ask, hopefully distracting him. He looks between us all, his eyes focusing on the old box on the floor, before he smiles at me.

"I didn't expect to find you out here. Having a little chat? Is there anything you need to tell the other masters about?" Master Pirate asks, and Hunter walks closer to me, standing at my side.

"Nothing, we have just missed each other and were planning a night in our rooms together," I say, making Master Pirate chuckle.

"You are not very good at distractions, but I will let it go for now, Master Cassandra," he says.

"I want to see this dragon I bought you so long ago," Hunter interrupts, and wraps a possessive arm around my waist, leading me away. Master Pirate follows, but Zack and Ryland stay behind. Zack holds the map in his hand, and winks at me when he catches my eye.

"Does your dragon have a name?" Master Pirate asks me as he steps up to my side, and Hunter pulls me even closer to him.

"Vivo," I say.

"A good, strong name," Master Pirate comments as we walk around a corner and past a massive group of people in cloaks. They all stop to stare, and then they bow their heads low.

"Before you ask, people will treat you this way from now on," Master Pirate informs me.

"They bow to someone they do not know, someone who has done nothing for them," I say, and Hunter squeezes me tightly to him.

"Yet," he whispers, and I look up at him as we walk. There is so much respect in his eyes, so much of something I don't know how to adequately return. His love is so much, so full of passion and desire that swirl in the darkness of him. It's everything in one emotionally charged look, and it's so hard to show him how I feel in return. A loud roar makes me sharply turn away to the three archways we are approaching, and towards Vivo, who is roaring at the people in front of her. They are trying to calm her down on the ledge outside. It looks like a landing bay, not too much different from where I initially landed, but it's not the same one. Vivo looks more and more distressed as the people hold their hands out, shouting for her to calm. Ice is all under her feet, melting slowly, yet more ice spreads over it every time she roars.

"Vivo," I shout, and her eyes turn towards me, locking onto me as I walk over. Master Pirate stays at the door, but Hunter stays at my side. When we get to her, I reach out and place my hand on her nose.

"I'm safe, but thank you for checking up on me,"

I say, and she huffs in response. "This is Hunter," I introduce him, and he slowly holds a hand out to her. She doesn't move, letting him place his hand next to mine.

"You like him, too? He is a little grumpy at times, but I think he just uses that to hide his sweet, loveable side," I say, and Hunter laughs.

"That's the first time anyone has called me sweet before, little bird," he responds, and I grin at him.

"Vivo, how about we show Hunter how this *little bird* can fly?" I ask her, and she roars her approval, while, for the first time ever, Hunter appears nervous.

"Woah now, I don't think flying is the best idea," Hunter says, stepping back, and I laugh.

"I'm shocked, is the big, bad Hunter scared of flying?" I ask, and he narrows his eyes at me.

"I'm not *scared* of flying," he snaps, but he doesn't frighten me like he would most people.

"Sure," I tease, grinning as I walk to the side of Vivo and start climbing. When I get to her spikes, I slide myself in between and stroke a hand down her back as I look down at Hunter.

"Come on. Don't let fear dictate what you do, and don't let it control you," I say gently. I'm surprised he is acting like this, I didn't expect it.

"It's not that, it's not even the flying. My father's dragon . . ." Hunter starts to say, but pauses, shaking his head. I give him a sympathetic look, and try to let my love shine through it. "The king used to make me ride her. She would drop me, then catch me with her claws. It was a game to them," he explains to me.

"Vivo would never do that, and we don't play games like him. I understand if you don't want to come, Hunter. You have nothing to prove to me . . . I don't think I could be near a fire again after what happened," I say quietly, but I know he can hear me.

"Look at us both, fearful of things that happened in our pasts . . . we are better than this. We are stronger than him," Hunter says, his voice strong as he walks over and climbs up Vivo, sliding in-between the spikes behind me and wrapping his arms around my waist.

"I love you," Hunter whispers in my ear, his voice ever so light. I turn to face him, keeping my hands on the spike in front of me.

"And I love you, my moody pirate," I say, and he kisses me, a harsh and demanding kiss that leaves me wanting more when he pulls away.

"I can't wait to get you alone, then it won't just be stolen kisses," he whispers against my lips. I gently run my lips across his and turn around, a massive smile on my face as I continue to stroke Vivo's neck.

"Let's go," I say, and she turns around, walking to the edge of the cliff and peering down. I feel Hunter's hands tighten on my waist, and she steps off the edge, diving down as I hold onto the spike in front of me for dear life. She suddenly opens her wings, and the wind shoots us up in the air as she glides around the mountain. When she evens herself out, I look around and notice her flying us in-between the mountains.

"Look," Hunter says behind me, letting go with one hand to quickly point to my left. I look over to see dozens of dragons flying around and baby dragons in nests on the other mountains. The dragons dive into the mountains from the top, so it must be their home in there.

"This is your home, isn't it?" I ask Vivo, who roars. I look back at the dragons, the red, yellow, and a few brown ones I can see. None of them look like Vivo, none of them are water or ice dragons.

"Not exactly your home then . . .," I say, and she whines a little.

"Water and ice dragons are usually born in the water, which is where those dragons typically live," he says.

"Then we will find her home somehow," I respond.

"Her home is with you; can't you see that? You are her rider, and where you go, so will she," he chuckles near my ear as I shiver. "It's a good thing you belong to pirates and the sea, isn't it?"

Chapter Seven

Cassandra

"**Y**ou got Hunter on a dragon? I'm impressed, Cass," Jacob says, as Vivo flies off. He walks out from one of the arches, coming to stand next to me and Hunter. I watch Vivo until she is out of sight before turning to face Jacob. His hair is messier than when I first met him, longer, but it looks good on him. The scar just adds to his looks in a way, but I regret that he had to lose sight in one of his eyes. He still smiles at me the same way he always has, like nothing has changed. He is my pirate that jumped off a ship for me, saved me, and with the help of his friends, showed me what it was like to actually live. In some ways, I owe all my happiness, my reason to fight for this world, to Jacob.

"Hunter bought her for me, so he had to fly with

her," I reply, with a grin when Hunter glares down at me.

"I was trying to impress you. I guess I didn't think it through at the time," he tells me, and I wrap an arm around his waist, leaning up to kiss his cheek.

"I was impressed," I whisper.

"I did come to find you for a reason," Jacob says, and I smile as I let go of Hunter and turn to him.

"So . . . you didn't just miss me?" I ask, teasing him a little. He steps closer, until his whole body is pressed to the front of mine as he speaks.

"You know I missed you, Cass," he whispers, and Hunter steps behind me, both of them keeping me tightly in between them.

"We both missed you, all of your pirates did," Hunter whispers next to my ear, before gently grazing his teeth on the outer shell, sending goose bumps through me.

"Sorry to interrupt, boys, but Cassy promised me some alone time. So, you will have to get in line," Everly's voice floats over to us, and she steps out of the shadows of the archway. Jacob leans down, kissing my forehead before stepping away.

"Hunter and I have new recruits to train, in fact, all of us are training today. Come to us when you can," Jacob says, and Hunter kisses my cheek, whispering to me before he moves back.

"My bed tonight, little bird." I watch him as he walks around me and past Everly. She has her arms crossed and an amused look on her face as she waits for my attention

"Glad to have some time alone with your pirates?" she asks me when I get to her, and she pulls me into a hug. I lean back, admiring her blonde hair that falls to her waist in perfect blonde curls and her big blue eyes.

"Yes, you could say that," I laugh, "you look amazing, so much better than when–" I stop talking when her face drops a little.

"I was starving then, I was weak and scared of everything that happened. I'm not that girl anymore," she turns slightly, so she's facing the side of the mountains. I turn following her gaze, seeing the view over the mountain; the stars slowly appearing behind the mountains and the peacefulness of the place. "I had to grow up and accept everything. Accept who I am in order to get my revenge, because if I lived in the past, there wouldn't be a future for me." She walks towards the archway, and I jog to catch up to her, walking at her side.

"We both have grown up a lot since this all

started. Neither of us had a choice, and we both want revenge," I say as we walk through the archway, and she turns down the right stone corridor, to a large set of stairs that go to the bottom floor.

"It's why we are friends, why the sea god brought us together. Our lives were never our own. We have always had a bigger price to pay to save Calais," she says, and walks down the stairs. A group of about ten children of varied ages see us and bow. When they look up, I see they are all changed ones.

"There are so many changed ones, but no females," I comment to Everly, not having an answer for her statement about our lives. She is right. Our lives were never our own. Yet, I wouldn't change anything about my life. It's lead me to where I am now. I hate my past with the king, his games and losing my father, but it made me who I am. I have the most important things in the world . . . my pirates. I feel like Everly would change everything about her past if she could, without a second thought.

"No, there are no female changed ones. The masters heard about what happened with the king from us when we got here. They didn't believe at first, but then the sea god spoke to them. Everything changed from then on. Everyone believes you are destined to save them, to save the sea," she says.

"No pressure then. I still have to find the true heir to put on the throne at the end of the war. I cannot be the one to rule," I reply, and then stop. "Look at this place, it's almost magical." Everly doesn't reply as I step off the bottom step of the stairs and into the forest of trees and plants of every colour. Every single thing growing here is so vibrant and beautiful. It's hard to look away from the brightness and life that is all around us. A man steps from behind a tree, walking over and bowing. When he straightens up, I see the changed mark that resembles a leaf on his forehead. The man has dark skin, brown eyes, and green vines wrapped around his arms and plain clothes.

"Welcome, Cassandra. The sea god told me I would meet you sometime soon. My name is Rikker, and I would very much love to speak to you if you have the time."

"At least he tells you things, I usually just get riddles," I say, making him laugh.

"The sea god is older than time, older than any other god, and I doubt he notices how he speaks. Even his children do not always understand every-thing he says," he says.

"Children?" I ask. "Do you mean changed ones? I've heard people say they are like his children."

"The sea god has many real children, many gods and goddesses that no one knows of, as well as many secrets," he says and winks at me. "That is a long story . . . another time perhaps, Master Cassandra?"

"Perhaps," I say, not wanting to worry about any other gods. The sea god has caused Calais enough problems. I smile at Rikker and look around.

"How is everything so healthy? Everywhere else the trees are dying, *Calais* is dying, and yet, it looks so *alive* here," I state.

"The changed ones help nature, it's what we were always meant to do. The world is dying because the natural balance is out," he says, and walks away, calling over his shoulder. "Come, Cassandra and Everleigh."

"No one calls me Everleigh. How did you know my full name?" Everly asks as we catch up to him, walking just behind him through the trees and plants.

"You know how I know, Everleigh," he chuckles, and I give Everly a confused look, but she isn't looking at me. She just stares at the floor, silent, her hair covering her face from me. When I reach over and squeeze her hand, she finally seems to snap out of it. But she only plasters a fake smile on her face as she moves her hand away. *What is going on with her?*

"My gift is to feel the emotions of plants, the ground, and even some animals, but that stretches my gifts," Rikker explains to me as he leans down, cupping a yellow-looking sprout in some soil. His hand starts to glow green–a warm glow–and I see his mark glowing the same colour. The glow fades away, and Rikker leans back on his knees.

"The sunflower is being killed by the tree. Its roots are making it impossible for the sunflower to grow," he says sadly and looks up at the tree. "Not that it is the tree's fault, it needs its roots to survive. Nature is like people in that aspect. We do what we must to survive, even if it costs the ones around us."

"How will you fix that, then?" I ask, knowing his words are about more than just the plants, but not calling him on it. He speaks in riddles like the sea god, but maybe Rikker has spent too much time talking to him to notice it.

"By moving the sunflower, of course," he responds like I'm stupid not to have come up with that answer on my own. As he stands up, I bite my tongue rather than replying. "I must be going now, but it was an honour to meet you, Cassandra."

"Maybe we can talk again? I would like to hear more about everything you know," I say honestly, and he bows his head.

"We will meet again, but not for a long time as you have more pressing matters," he says with a look of worry flashing over his face. He walks off before I can say anything.

"The changed ones here are weird," Everly says, nudging my shoulder and making me laugh.

"I think they all speak to gods, and they have powers. That would make anybody weird," I say and turn to Everly. "What was it you wanted to tell me?" I ask as I suddenly feel worry, anger, and upset through my bond. I can't say anything, and I have no idea who it came from. I try to feel for the bond, but Everly distracts me, and it goes away.

"Not here, but my room isn't far," she says, nodding her head to the left. We walk through the trees and plants, and as we come out on the other side, I see Chaz looking around. He sees me and Everly and comes running over. The closer he gets, the more worried I become.

"Laura isn't well, and a changed one who can heal is trying to help her now. Hunter and Ryland need you at their side," Chaz says, keeping his voice quiet, so the people walking around us can't hear.

"What do you mean she isn't well? What happened?"

"Laura is old, and hasn't been well since we

escaped the castle. I don't know how to explain it, but it was like her soul was crushed. Her body started to give up not long after. We have kept her on bed rest, which she never argued with, and today she is much worse. I fear there is nothing anyone can do now," Chaz tells me. I look over at Everly, who nods.

"Go, what I have to talk to you about can wait," she says, and I slide my hand into Chaz's, letting him lead me away.

Chapter Eight

Cassandra

"Ry," I say gently, placing my hand on his shoulder as I step into the room. Chaz closes the door behind me. He turns, letting me into the room where Hunter is sitting on a chair next to a small bed. Laura lies on the bed looking pale and much older than I remember from when I saw her last. Master Light has his hand on the top of Laura's head, and it's glowing a white colour like the light coming from his eyes. I don't say anything while we wait, just stay at Ryland's side. He just stands deathly still, watching, waiting. Master Light finally pulls his hand away, patting Laura's arm and stepping away.

"Can I speak to both of you outside?" Master Light asks Hunter and Ryland carefully.

"I'm not a child. Tell me what you have figured out," Laura coughs out.

"Nothing you are not aware of, Lauraina. You must be in great pain, and you have hidden it so well," Master Light says quietly to her, and she turns away.

"Little bird, will you stay with her while we walk Master Light out?" Hunter asks me, and I nod, walking over and sitting in the seat he vacates. He walks out of the room with Ryland and Master Light following.

"Riah? Is that you?" Laura asks, reaching for my hand and rolling her head to look at me.

"No, Laura, it's Cassandra," I reply lightly, letting her grab my hand tightly, and she locks her blue eyes with mine.

"It's nearly time, and I wish Riah was here," she says, her voice so full of despair that it is heartbreaking. "I wish my little girl was here." Her words are spoken so softly, so full of a longing for a child that is a child no more.

"At least in death, I will know my grandsons are safe. That if the king burns the world away, their souls will always be chosen," she wheezes out.

"You should rest, Laura," I comment.

"They say my daughter is mad, that she speaks to

ghosts all the time," Laura shakes her head, "I say that she isn't."

"Ghosts? The souls of her chosen?" I ask, replaying what she has just said about Hunter and Ryland's souls.

"Even if someone burns away the body of a chosen . . . chosen never leave their changed one," she whispers, "or I believe their souls never do. Not until their changed one is dead. Soul mates cannot be parted, remember that, Cassandra." She coughs, blood dripping out from the corner of her lips. I reach for a cloth that is off to the side, wiping the blood away. She grabs my arm, with a strength I didn't think she had left and holds on tight, pulling me down, so our faces are close together.

"Give my daughter peace," she says, letting go as the door is opened and falling back on the bed. Her eyes close, almost like she never moved. I feel Ryland and Hunter come to my sides, both placing a hand on her. A wave of grief slams into me through the bond and overwhelms me, making tears fall from my eyes. I'm not sure which brother the grief is coming from, but it's so sad either way. I just want to hold them both and tell them she isn't in pain anymore.

"She is gone, isn't she?" Hunter is the first to speak after a long time.

"She is with the sea god, at peace finally," I say the only words that feel right. Ryland walks out of the room, slamming the door, and I move to follow when Hunter grabs my arm.

"Let him be. He needs to be alone, to settle his thoughts. Trust me, little bird," he assures me. Releasing me, Hunter leans down to kiss Laura's forehead lightly.

"I never had a mother, and I never told you, but I was lucky to have you. I wouldn't have survived without your guidance and love. You rest now. Your fight is over, but I will finish it while you rest in peace," he says, standing up straight and walking out of the room with me following him. I hold a hand up to Chaz and Jacob outside and make it clear with one look that they aren't to follow us right now.

"Leave me be, little bird," Hunter warns as I get to his side.

"You can't push me away. Neither can Ryland, but he needs his time alone. I am not going anywhere," I say, and Hunter narrows his eyes on me as he suddenly stops.

"Leave," he demands, making the single word snarky and cruel. I cross my arms, glaring right back and not backing down. He doesn't say a word, turning and walking away. I keep about two steps behind him as he walks down the stone paths, pushing people out of his way as he goes. He turns a sharp left, going towards the waterfall. I can see a small cave to the left of it as we get closer. Hunter walks straight into the dark cave, and I follow, using my hands to feel around the cave until I see the light on the other side. We come out into a massive cave and inside is a giant lake with hundreds of ships drifting. They all have their sails down, though none are moving. I can see the lake leads to a long river on the other side, which must in turn, lead out of the mountains. I look around and see Hunter walk over to a ship near the back of the fleet, small lanterns lit up on the deck. There is no one around, not that I can see, at least. I follow him, but stop abruptly when I see our ship. It feels like it's been forever since I've been on board this ship, since I was stolen from it. Now that it's next to others, I can see it's one of the biggest and most well-built. It still looks shiny, and any damage that was done when I was taken has been repaired, to the point that I wouldn't know anything had happened to the ship. I run to catch up, and watch Hunter jump onto a rope hanging off the ship and climb up it like a monkey. *How am I meant to do that?*

"Cassandra?" a timid male voice comes from

next to me, and I turn to see Roger walking over, pulling his cloak back. He looks so much older than when we last saw each other. He is taller, his brown hair is longer and curlier, and his baby face is lost to an older look. He is going to be a heartbreaker in a few years, that's for sure.

"Roger," I say fondly, pulling him into a small hug when he gets near.

"They said Livvy is dead, that she betrayed you . . . I, I don't know how she could have done that to you," he blurts out and then looks away, "I thought she loved me, and that she loved you like a sister. Her home was with us, and she destroyed that."

"Roger," I say gently, placing my hand on his shoulder and he turns, waiting for me to say something I'm not sure how to say.

"Everyone makes decisions, good and bad. Livvy made hers, and it cost her life. She has paid enough, and only the sea god can decide her punishment in death," I say. I can't forgive her for what she did, but there is no point in hating the dead.

"I miss her, despite everything . . . I miss her," he says and looks up at the ship.

"I miss her, too, even if I hate to admit it," I tell him, being honest, though the words sting as they come out of my lips.

"If you want to get on the ship, there is a net near the front. I use it to bring food to Salty Sam every day," he explains and reaches into his cloak, pulling out a small bag of cat food.

"I will feed him," I say, and he hands me the bag and pats my shoulder before walking away. I watch him leave, knowing there are no words that could make what Livvy did better for him. It's something he needs to accept, much like I do at some point. I guess I've just denied it for as long as possible, tried to make it easier on my heart because I did care for her. I slide the bag of food into my pocket, barely able to make it fit. Walking towards the front of the ship, I find where the net is hanging down and tied to the dock. I step onto it, climbing up slowly and trying my hardest not to fall. I get to the top, pull myself over, and flop onto the other side, landing on my back.

"Ouch," I huff, lifting myself up off the floor and looking around. Hunter is standing in front of the wheel, holding it tightly in his hand, and his head bowed down. I pull the food out my pocket, open the bag, and leave it on the floor, knowing the evil cat will find it on his own. Every step I take towards Hunter, seems to echo something deep inside of me. Maybe it's our bond, maybe it's just because I love him, but I seem to be able to feel his pain like it's my own. I get to his side, not knowing what to say, how to tell him anything. I slide myself under his arm, in between him and the wheel, so it presses into my back.

"Talk to me, my dark pirate," I whisper, sliding my hands onto either side of his face and lifting his head up. I can feel the tears under my palms, but I don't say a word as he locks his eyes onto mine. There is so much pain in them. There is a turmoil of emotion swirling in his dark eyes. It feels like I could drown in the depth of them, knowing I wouldn't fight it or even try to save myself.

"For the second time in my entire life, I feel powerless. I feel like the pain inside of me is trying to choke me," he finally says, his eyes locked with mine the whole time. He isn't running from me, that's one bonus.

"When I lost my father in the games, the pain was indescribable. I don't remember much from those last moments, other than the pain. I know it won't go away. I know I will have to live with the pain, but time does help," I reply to him in a gentle voice.

"I know I have to lose my mother, just after I've

lost the woman who brought me up," he whispers. I hate seeing him like this, my strong pirate.

"You know Riah has to die?" I whisper back.

"I've always known it. It's the only way to stop my father. Ryland knows it, too. We have made a plan and we will do it together. She deserves to have her sons with her as she dies," he says, but his voice catches on his words. He can't even say them, let alone do it. I won't let him or Ryland put themselves in that position. No one should have to kill their own mother.

"I know Laura is gone, and that you feel alone, but you are not. You have me, and you have a family that loves you," I say, and he grabs my hands, pinning them to the wheel on each side of my head and pressing his body into mine.

"Say it, little bird," he demands, moving his face close to mine, so there is nowhere else I could look. Not that I could look away from him right now, not when he is showing me this vulnerable side to him.

"I love you," I say each word slowly, but his lips part subtly, his eyes closing like my words alone are pleasurable to him.

"And I love you, my little bird," he says when he opens his eyes, and seconds later he slams his lips onto mine. I lose any control of my emotions, my desires, as he rips my clothes away. He kisses his way down my naked body, taking his time to kiss each nipple thoroughly, before gently biting and mixing the pain with the sweet pleasure. I gasp when his mouth finds my core, his tongue swirling around my nub with a skill that send me over the edge in seconds. Hunter rises up, shoving his trousers down and lifting me up, pushing my body against the wheel as he slides deep inside of me.

"Hunter," I moan, having no control over my voice as he pounds into me again and again, filling me in a way that I know I will never forget.

"Cassandra," he groans, biting down and sucking on my neck as he finishes, sending waves of pleasure through me at the same time. We stare at each other, both of us breathless and trying to gain our breaths back.

"How about we go down to my cabin, and really make this ship rock?" he whispers against my lips, sucking my bottom lip into his mouth and biting down before releasing.

"Good plan, my dark pirate," I grin, and kiss him as he carries us away.

Chapter Nine

Ryland

"Ryland?" Chaz's voice comes over to me, and I look up from the tree I'm leaning against to see him walking over. His gaze drifts from me, to the stone wall next to me, and down to my hands. Blood drips from my knuckles onto the grass, but the pain is almost soothing at this point. Laura, the only real parent I have ever had, is dead. Her soul is at peace, but all I feel is anger. His hands are tucked into his pockets, his blond hair pushed all over the place. He stops next to me, silently supporting me without saying anything. I'm glad Cassandra didn't follow me, I couldn't deal with anyone near me for a while. I'm not sure I even want Chaz near me.

"Is she with Hunter?" I ask, needing to know my brother isn't alone.

"Of course she is, but I'm sure she will be on her way to find you soon," he says, and I laugh hoarsely.

"I'm in no state to see her," I reply.

"Do you think she would judge you?" he asks,

"No, but she deserves better," I respond.

"You *are* better," he tells me, his voice firm, but I don't know if I can completely believe him.

"When we die, do you believe we go to the sea god and then have peace?" I ask Chaz, wanting to know his opinion.

"Come with me, I want to show you something," Chaz says and walks off. I follow him, ignoring the stares of people we pass. He opens a door near the entrance to the mountains, though not one I've ever entered before.

"What is this place?" I ask Chaz when I follow him into the oval cave. There are hundreds of lit and unlit candles on the floor, high lightening the drawings on the walls.

"History of Calais, more specifically, of the gods. These are some of the earliest drawings anyone knows of," Chaz explains and lifts a candle up, holding it to the wall to my left. There are drawings of a man walking out of the water, streams of water flying everywhere. Next to it is a drawing of a man kissing the forehead of a baby lying in a mother's arms.

"I've examined these drawings many times, and this is what they say about death," Chaz says, nodding his head right to the middle of the cave. There's a drawing of a woman on the floor, an outline of a body flying out of her. The next drawing shows a choice, with two men holding out their hands. One looks like he is in the sea, and the other looks like he is in flames.

"This is the sea god, but who is that?" I ask, pointing at the man in the flames.

"The sea god wasn't the only god born, they say he has a brother. The god of souls, that is who is standing there," he explains to me. I've never heard of the god of souls, but it would make sense there is more than one god if it's possible to have one.

"More gods? Don't we have enough problems with just the one?" I muse.

"Yes," he chuckles, "but there isn't proof that the god of souls actually exists, just drawings."

"What does the god of souls do?" I ask.

"Drags the evil and undeserving souls into the deepest fires so that they may never be re-born, never know peace," he says, and there's a cold chill in the air as I think on his words. It's probably wrong that the first thing I think of is how I hope when my father dies, he meets the god of souls.

"And the deserving?" I ask.

"Know eternal peace, safe in the hands of the sea god," he says, and I nod. "People come here to light a candle in memory of those they have lost. Perhaps this could be your way of saying goodbye?" he suggests.

I think over his words and walk to the middle of the room, falling to my knees on the cold stone. I pick up an unlit candle, lighting it with the tip of another and placing it down in the middle of so many others.

"I can only remember you in my earliest memories, Laura, not my mother, not my father, or even Hunter. Just memories of you holding me as I cried, of you telling me silly fairy tales, and even times you told me off for pushing my luck. You were a true parent to me, and you deserved a long life of peace. I hope the sea god is with you now, taking you somewhere peaceful. We will see each other again one day. I love you, Laura, rest well with the gods and give them trouble with that stick of yours," I say, roughly wiping away a tear that falls down my cheek before standing up.

"I'm going to miss getting hit with that stick. I

hope she has a stick in the afterlife and hits the sea god with it for keeping Cassandra from us for so long," Chaz says, making me laugh a little. Chaz did the right thing bringing me here, giving me the chance to say goodbye, and to remember Laura as she truly was.

"Thank you for bringing me here, it's just what I needed. You are a good friend, Chaz," I say, and he chuckles.

"Friend? Or more like a brother who's not related by blood?" he inquires, walking to the door and opening it as I smile.

"Brother, then." I walk past him, waiting for him to shut the door behind me.

"Now, let's go back to my room and sort your hands out before our girl finds you in this state," he says, patting my shoulder.

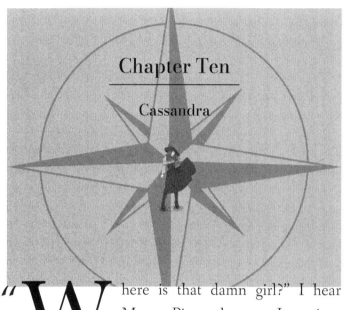

Chapter Ten

Cassandra

"Where is that damn girl?" I hear Master Pirate shout, as I run into the training room with Hunter at my side. He isn't running, just strolling behind me and stops at my side in front of Master Pirate, who doesn't look impressed one bit. I smooth down my messy hair, untidy clothes and flushed cheeks. I woke up on the ship, knowing I would be late, but Hunter had no plan on letting me out of that bed. *Not that I'm complaining.*

"That *damn girl* is my fiancé, and unless you want me slamming my fist into your face, be more respectful," Hunter drawls in a surprisingly calm voice. Master Pirate and Hunter stare at each other, before Master Pirate nods.

"Understood," he remarks, looking over at me. His black hair is tied at the back of his head, and his eyes are narrowed on me like I've just killed his cat or something. He is still as huge as I remember, but his cloak is gone, and it shows off his impressive body.

"Have fun, I will check in on Ryland. Don't kill Master Asshole, yeah?" Hunter requests, making me chuckle as he pulls me to him and kisses me deeply. I'm breathless by the time he pulls away and leaves me on shaky legs. Master Pirate glares at Hunter as he walks away, before turning his eyes back to me.

"What's your first name? I don't like calling you master whatever," I ask him, wanting to know.

"Master Pirate *is* my name," he replies dryly.

"It's going to be your first name, or master asshole . . . your choice?" I push, crossing my arms.

"If you beat me, I will tell you my name, Cassandra," he suggests. The smirk on his lips makes me think he believes he won't have to tell me.

"You think you will win?"

"From what I've heard, you have no control. Your power reacts due to stress, which is the starting base of our powers," he tells me, and holds his arms behind his back as he starts walking around me in a circle.

"Water is your gift, like mine, and when

controlled properly, is the most powerful gift any changed one can have," he tells me.

"Why is that? I assumed fire was the most powerful," I comment, and he arches a blond eyebrow at me.

"Fire can be put out, while water cannot be stopped, only controlled," he says and stops right in front of me.

"Water," he comments, lifting both his hands up and a long stream of water streams out from them, shooting up into the air as I take a step back. The water swirls around, getting faster and faster, until it looks more like a water tornado. Master Pirate lets it go, and it falls to the floor, but he keeps one hand in the air, still controlling it as it swirls around.

"Amazing," I say, actually meaning it.

"I can make this, but only with this amount of water. I've heard you flooded an entire room, am I right?" he enquires.

"Yes," I say, folding my arms and watching as he stops the water, letting it splash all over the floor and soaking my trousers.

"Then if we can teach you control, you would be stronger than any changed one I have ever trained," he states.

"I can't seem to call the water at will. It only

responds when I'm in danger," I explain. He nods, sitting on the floor.

"Sit down," he instructs and I do, ignoring the cold water soaking my bottom through my trousers.

"Close your eyes, Cassandra," he tells me, and I raise an eyebrow at him, before doing as he asks.

"Now what?" I ask.

"Our power comes from our chosen. I have one chosen, so my power is limited to her, but our bond is so strong that I can hear her thoughts. I can sense where she is without opening my eyes, and if she were in pain, I would know," he tells me.

"My bond isn't that strong," I say.

"It is strong, but still new and muddled because you have so many chosen. It's rare for a changed one to take so many chosen. In fact, there is only one changed that I know of that even has four chosen, not six like you have taken," he informs me, but his voice holds no judgement, only stating a fact. I wonder why he doesn't mention the queen, as she had four chosen. I hate how everyone here just seems to have forgotten her.

"Are you saying I won't ever have that bond?" I ask him, keeping my eyes closed. I don't want to hear the answer. It really doesn't matter in the end, because I wouldn't change anything.

"Not at all, you will have that bond with each of them in a few years. Maybe an even more powerful bond than any of us have experienced," he says.

"Right, so why are we closing our eyes as we speak?" I ask.

"Straight to the point, no thank you for the reassurance and advice?" he asks me, but it's clear he doesn't want a reply as he keeps speaking. "Our power comes from our bond; it's where it builds, where it comes from. Imagine your bond as you listen to my words." I take a deep breath, doing as he asks and feeling for the bond. It's like a warm place in my chest, where I can sense my pirates and their love and trust.

"Now, imagine a need to protect that bond, like a wave of water covering it," he says, and I do as he asks, feeling water spreading out from my hands. I hold them with my palms facing the floor as I keep the feeling of my bond in the forefront of my mind and the need to protect it.

"Open your eyes, Cassandra," he tells me, and I blink in shock when I see the entire room flooded in a low level of water. We are in a clearing; the water doesn't touch us at all.

"You have so much control of this water, it is yours. You have made it so it doesn't even touch us.

Now lift it into the air, high enough to touch the ceiling," Master Pirate demands.

"I-I can't do that," I stutter out.

"Now, Cassandra. Don't think about it, just feel," he pushes me, placing a hand over his heart. I close my eyes, trusting my bond, and try to picture all of the water rising. It's hard to imagine the impossible, but I have to trust that I'm strong enough to do just that. A warm feeling spreads all over me, and I open my eyes, knowing if I were to look up, the water would be floating.

"Look," Master Pirate says, and I nod my head before looking up at the ceiling, where all the water floats. It's easy once you can control it, like it listens to my demands. My love for my pirates makes this possible. I stand up, holding my hands in the air, and push all the water into three balls.

"Let's play," I grin, stepping back as Master Pirate laughs, and I throw one of the balls of water at him. He goes flying across the floor, somehow landing on his feet, but dripping wet. He holds his hands out at his side, and two balls of water appearing like mine. I pull my own spheres of water right in front of me, and aim another one at him. His own water sphere meets mine, and he follows straight after with a jet of water aimed right at me. I quickly make my last sphere of water into a jet, and it collides with his directly in between the two of us. I have to hold both my hands up, struggling to push against the pressure from his water. It inches towards me, and I'm gradually losing ground, one step back at a time. I can't lose this, I need to prove to him that I'm not nothing. *Nothing.* The word evokes memories of the king and his dark, evil eyes. The amount of hate in his sure expression when he said I was nothing flashes in my mind. I channel the hate, opening my eyes, and suddenly everything changes. My jet of water extends, getting stronger and destroys his, blasting into him and this time, slamming him into the wall. I look down, realising I'm actually hovering above the ground as water swirls around me. The power disappears quickly, and I collapse onto the wet floor. The door opens behind me, and Dante and Everly walk in. They both stop, looking at me, and then over to Master Pirate. Everly runs over to check on Master Pirate as Dante comes to me, offering me a hand. He pulls me up and holds me close.

"Are you alright, pretty girl?" he asks me, pulling back and checking me over.

"I'm fine, it was just training. I needed a changed one's help to learn," I explain to him.

"You just scared me, seeing you lying on the floor like that," he says, and I wrap my arms around him.

"I'm sorry," I mumble, and he kisses the top of my head. I look over as we hear clapping, slow loud claps. Master Pirate walks over to us, with Everly at his side, who looks amused.

"So, I won, what's your name?" I ask.

"Never trust a pirate, Cassandra. Hasn't anyone ever told you that?" Master Pirate taunts. He walks around me and out the door as I laugh. Everly leaves with Master Pirate, shutting the door behind them.

"I missed you, but didn't quite expect to see this when I walked in," Dante says, sliding his hand into my hair.

"I didn't know I could even do this," I admit. "It's amazing to have such a connection to water."

"It's amazing to be so close to you, and to be able to watch you be so wonderful," he says, being the charmer that I've always known he was. I chuckle, leaning up and kissing him slowly, taking my time teasing him. He allows it for a second, before grabbing my face with his hands and taking over.

"Tease," he whispers against my lips.

"You're *my* pirate, am I not allowed to tease you?" I ask, running my hand down his hard chest, and he catches it, bringing it to his lips.

"As much as I want to lay you on this floor, take off your clothes, and make you moan in that sweet way I know you do, I can't. This is a public training room, and I have a class due in here at any moment," he says and just as he speaks, the door opens behind him.

"Fine, can I stay and watch for a bit?" I ask, and he nods.

"Sure, you could even join in if you wanted?"

"No, I'm no fighter, but I have other talents," I grin, and his eyes drift down my body as I step away.

"You sure do," he drawls in a seductive tone that makes me long to be alone with him. Ten men and three women come in to the class as I wait, and they all look at Dante like he is their god or something. They all appear shocked to see me sitting on the sidelines, but they don't say a word. I watch as Dante takes control of the class, teaching them how to use a sword and how to throw daggers. He encourages them to practice fighting in pairs with wooden swords to start with. While they are all practising, Dante walks over to me, sitting down.

"You're a good teacher. They all seem to respect you."

"I've been teaching them for a year, that's why," he shrugs like it's nothing.

"You've helped them and given them a strength they can use to avenge whoever they are fighting for. Everyone must have lost something, like a home, or worse, someone," I muse, and Dante slides his hand into mine.

"Loss makes us stronger, and it gives us a reason to fight. We can do this," he says and gets up, going back to his students.

Chapter Eleven

Cassandra

"Can I steal Cassandra from you?" Jacob asks as Dante and I walk out of the training room holding hands. Dante lifts my hand, kissing the back of it before letting go.

"Of course, but I want her back tonight," Dante replies, keeping his eyes on mine before he turns and walks away. Jacob holds his hand out for me, and I accept it as I look him over. He has a blue shirt on today, and the buttons are done up to his chest, except the top one. The shirt is tucked into black trousers that are tight and show off his muscular thighs. I let my eyes drift up to his messy brown hair, the scar I want so much to make right for him, and finally to his warm blue eyes.

"Why did you get rid of your beard? I kind of miss it," I ask, reaching with my spare hand to his shaven face.

"I didn't know you liked my beard. I guess I might have to grow it back," he cheekily says, "but for now, I have a surprise for you." He lets go of my hand to wrap an arm around my waist and guide me down the corridor.

"Will you tell me what happened when you were at the castle before? Chaz told me once that you had to leave your parents and escape, but not why."

"I saved a child's life, a child who did nothing other than save his brother."

"What happened?" I ask.

"We received news that a changed one had been hidden and he was older, around eight. I went to the ship with the other guards to collect the changed one. When we got there, we soon realised the changed one's twin brother had drawn a mark on his forehead and switched places with him. The king ordered the boy to be killed, and I couldn't allow it. He was eight years old and only wanted to save his brother," he stops.

"So, you helped him escape?"

"Yes, but the king thought it was another guard that helped him and killed him before I could save his life and say it was me. Even though I saved the child, I still killed the guard," he laments. I lift his hand, kissing his knuckles.

"For what it's worth, I believe you did the right thing."

"Maybe, maybe not. I try not to dwell on the past and my mistakes anymore," he tells me.

"Thank you for telling me," I say gently.

"I would tell you anything you ask of me. There are no secrets between us," he says. We pass several people, who stop to lower their heads.

"I wish they wouldn't do that," I tell Jacob, who waits until we pass them and walk down the stairs before he replies.

"Is it that bad to be respected?"

"No, but only a royal should be bowed to,"

"Or their saviour. They believe in you, like I do, like I always have, Cass," he tells me. I sigh, resting my head against the side of his chest as we walk down another hallway. I start to hear running water ahead, even though the waterfall is right behind us. The small hallway stops with a long row of stairs that travel down. We walk down slowly, letting go of each other to walk one at a time down the narrow stair-well. When Jacob moves out of the way, I can see a giant pool in the room. There's a ledge, and it's cut out of the mountain, where the water falls down the side. The moonlight lights the room up, reflecting off the pool of water. It's so stunning that I don't want to move, just observe.

"I'm going to teach you how to swim," Jacob states, and I turn around, watching him slowly unbutton his shirt.

"Really?" I breathe out. I've always wanted to learn, but until now, it's never been a possibility.

"Yes, learning to swim is something you need to know. I want to help you," he tells me and pulls his shirt off. "Are you going to get undressed, Cass?" he asks, making my cheeks redden. Too busy staring at his chest, I'm distracted. I trail my eyes over his muscular body, following the dark line of chest hair that looks so soft and tantalizingly dips into his trousers.

"Err . . . yes," I mumble, and turn around, walking to a nearby rock. I pull my boots and trousers off first, followed by my shirt. I turn around, standing in just a small vest and underwear, which does little to hide my body from Jacob. Not that I want to hide anything from him. Without warning, he suddenly dives into the water.

"Beautiful. Just watching you standing there, the moonlight reflecting off your pale skin, your hazel eyes almost glowing; you are just so beautiful, Cassandra," he tells me, making my breath catch in my throat. I wait for him to reappear, watching as his head and chest break free of the water. If I thought he looked amazing in just his underwear before, it's nothing compared to the dripping wet look he is currently sporting.

"We will never teach you to swim if you keep looking at me like that," Jacob jokes, with a smirk on his lips. I chuckle, walking to the edge and sitting down as I dangle my legs in the slightly cold water. Jacob swims to me, resting his hands on my knees.

"Trust me?" he asks, and I nod, placing my hand on his cheek.

"Always," I reply, letting him pull me into the water. I wrap my legs around him, as he splays his hands on my back. My vest stops him from actually touching me, and I wish I'd taken it off now.

"Swimming is fairly easy. It's just certain arm movements, and kicking your legs. This pool is deep, so I will stay close to you," he says, pushing me away from him a little.

"Float on your stomach?" he asks, placing a hand on my stomach as I float forward and try not to get any water in my mouth. Jacobs explains the basics of how to swim. I follow his directions, and he keeps a hand on my stomach the entire time.

"Can I let go?" he asks.

"What if I don't want you to?" I ask, pushing back and pressing my back against his chest. He pulls me close, his head resting against my ear.

"Are you sure you want that?" he asks me, his words low and seductive as he presses his hard body against my back.

"Jacob, I love you. I'm always sure," I tell him. He turns me quickly to face him, pressing his lips to mine. He swims us backwards as we kiss, until my back hits the wall. I use the rocks I can feel to hold my one leg up and wrap the other around his as we kiss until neither of us can think straight. Jacob slides his warm hand under my top, flicking a finger over my hard nipple and gently pinching, making me gasp against his lips.

"No more teasing, I need you," I mutter, making him chuckle low.

"Trust me, I need you more. But I want to get to know your body. I want to feel you come around my fingers before I get inside of you," he whispers, biting my lip as he slides his hand out my top. He rips my underwear off me, making me gasp, and then he slowly inches two fingers inside of me.

"Hold on to me," he tells me, before letting go of my hip with his spare hand, and roughly pulling my top down. Jacob ducks his head underwater; his fingers start moving in and out of me as he sucks my nipple into his mouth. I moan as his thumb finds my nub and rubs circles, sending me over the edge, with a loud scream. Jacob lets go of me, only to widen my legs with his hips and pull his head out of the water, sliding into me with one long stroke.

"Oh, gods, Cass," he mutters, thrusting in and out of me, leaving me no break to catch my breath. I fling my head back, getting closer and closer to the edge, and see Chaz leaning against the wall by the door. Seeing him there, watching us, shocks me a little, but Jacob doesn't seem to notice as his lips find my nipple once more, and his thrusts pick up speed. I keep my eyes locked with Chaz as I finish, a long moan slipping out through my lips, and Jacob groans out his release a few seconds later. I move my eyes back to Jacob, who looks away from me towards Chaz, but doesn't seem bothered to see him there.

"Are you going to join us?" Jacob asks Chaz, as he slides out of me, and I miss the feeling already.

"Cassandra?" Chaz asks, and I turn, locking eyes with him as I nod. Chaz walks into the room, slowly removing his clothes, but never looking away from me as I take him all in. He isn't as muscular as the other pirates, but his smaller waist shows off a long V shape and an impressive length underneath. He has some pale blond hair on his chest, and a few scars on the tops of his arms. Chaz keeps only his shell necklace on as he gets into the water, swimming towards me.

"Go to him," Jacob whispers in my ear, making me blush. I swim carefully over to Chaz, who catches me in his arms and holds me to him, his length pushing up against me.

"You can swim," he says, grinning.

"Yes," is all I can reply, as Chaz lines us up. One move and he would be inside of me. Chaz holds my hips with his hands, stopping me from sinking down on him.

"You can tell me no, but it needs to be now," he breathes against my lips, loosening his grip on my hips a little. Instead of replying, I drop down on his length, letting him fill me, and he gasps at the same time I do.

"Doesn't she feel amazing?" I hear Jacob ask. Suddenly I feel his hands slide around my chest, grabbing my breasts and playing with my nipples as Chaz moves in and out of me.

"Amazing is an understatement," Chaz groans. I moan out as Jacob slides a finger over my nub and Chaz kisses me harshly. The motion of Jacob's expert hands, Chaz being inside of me, and everything I'm feeling sends me crashing over the edge. Chaz shouts my name as he finishes, holding me close as I wait to be able to speak.

"No words," I manage to gasp.

"Speechless, I like that," Chaz says, and we all chuckle. Chaz pulls out of me, and swims us over to the edge, which we all rest against. I hold Jacob's hand as I relax in Chaz's arms. This moment is perfect.

"I hate to ruin this moment, but I did come to find you for another reason," Chaz says, like he just remembered.

"Huh?"

"The masters have called an emergency meeting tonight. You have about an hour, or maybe less now," he tells me, and I huff.

"So, staying in this pool all day isn't an option?" I ask, making them both groan.

"If you keep talking like that, we won't be getting

out of this pool," Jacob says, letting go of my hand and pulling himself out the water. I trail my eyes over his naked body, his toned back and bottom, and wish we didn't have responsibilities.

Maybe one day, we won't.

Chapter Twelve

Cassandra

"Ry?" I ask quietly when I see him for the first time since Laura died. I tried looking for him before training and then the pool, but had no luck. Ry is leaning against the bridge, his head bowed.

"Can you give us a few minutes?" I ask Chaz and Jacob, who nod and walk away after giving me loving looks. I walk up to Ryland, placing my hands on his face and lifting his head, so he will look at me.

"Ry?" I repeat as his blue eyes meet mine.

"I'm sorry if I ignored you; I just needed time to process her death. I still can't believe she is gone," he says.

"Don't apologize. I'm the one who should be sorry for not finding you quicker," I say.

"You shouldn't be," he chuckles and pulls me into his arms.

"What did Laura say to you before she . . ." he asks me, trailing off.

"To give her daughter peace," I tell him honestly.

"Something I fully expected from her," he says gruffly, and leans down, kissing me. His hands slide into my hair as we kiss, and I hold onto his jacket, enjoying this peaceful moment between us.

"You should go to the meeting," he says as he breaks away from our kiss. "My sadness and grief won't be lost in a moment, but in a death. The death of my father, the man who caused all this,"

"What do you see for our future, Ryland?" I ask, wanting to distract him if only for a second.

"All of us, on our ship, free. Maybe even a baby or two to hold," he says, chuckling at my shocked expression.

"A baby? I didn't know you wanted children," I say.

"I never did until I met you. We would have stunning children, wearing little pirate hats and causing trouble," he grins, and kisses my cheek. "Go before your cheeks burn any brighter." I grin and turn around, walking to the bridge. As I step onto the bridge, I feel its power wash over me. I continue my walk across, but pause when I get to the middle, hearing a noise. I look around, spinning in a circle to see where the noise came from.

"*Cassandra . . . leave the mountain. No time,*" the Sea God whispers, and I fall to my knees, holding my hands to my head. The pain from his words echoing in my mind make it feel like my head may explode.

"*Leave, Cassandra, leave now,*" he demands, and then the voice drifts away, like it was never there. I have to lie on the bridge floor for a while, feeling lost and in pain. When the pain leaves, and it's reduced to just a dull ache, I manage to get up. *I wish he would stop making demands.* I walk the final part across the bridge, feeling better with every step.

"I heard there was a meeting?" I ask as I step off the bridge, and see only Master Light waiting for me in the cave room. He has a white cloak on today, and his tired eyes meet mine across the crystal table.

"Yes, the others will join us shortly. We have a problem that we did not expect," he tells me as I step closer, and see his pinched face. "Please sit down, Master Cassandra." I do as he asks, and we wait silently for the others to come. Master Pirate comes into the room, sitting down with a huff and a face full of annoyance.

"We should begin, the others won't be here for a

long while with everything that is happening," Master Pirate says, and Master Light nods, switching his gaze to me.

"You must leave the mountains," he tells me simply.

"What?" I ask, surprised.

"Three hours ago, a ship came to us. All but one of the king's guards on board were dead. The entire ship was full of guards that had sided with the rebellion, every single one of them. The king knew exactly who had betrayed him, which causes everything we have been told by the guards to be compromised. We only know this, because he left this one guard alive to send a message to us," he sighs.

"What was the message?" I ask carefully.

"The king has an army ready, armed with three hundred ships. He is coming to the mountains in one month's time, when the councils have been ordered to send him more fighters. He will come in, riding his dragon, and destroy this place. He knows you are here, Cassandra. Someone in the mountains must have betrayed us," Master Pirate growls out. "I will find out who and have their head for the betrayal, but the mountains are no longer safe for you."

"That's why you think I need to leave?" I ask, but the question pretty much answers itself.

"Do you think the sea god only tells you things? Whispers only to you? We know of the map and the crown that lies with the mermaids. You must learn to trust us, Cassandra. In time, I hope that happens," Master Light chides and stands up. He walks over to me, sitting on my desk, and placing a hand on my shoulder.

"The deal must be completed, and I know you can see this through. We will ride across the storm sea in three weeks. You have three weeks to travel to the mermaids, and get that crown," he tells me. Master Pirate locks eyes with me.

"Cassandra, the crown will make your power rival his. For all the pain and death he has caused, make sure he dies for it. Do not second guess yourself. I believe in you," he tells me, and I smile.

"Didn't know you could be so nice, Master Pirate," I say.

"Not nice, I just don't want to die, and you are the only way to secure my survival for the foreseeable future," he tells me. His cold, aloof expression is back, but I think it's only a way to hide that he can be nice when he wants. "I have found five men to travel with your pirates and help run the ship. They are all very trustworthy and brilliant fighters, which you may need."

"Thank you. I best go and tell my chosen the plan," I say, sliding out of my seat.

"Make sure the girl goes with you," Master Light's demand stops me before I can walk out of the door.

"What girl?" I inquire.

"The future queen," Master Light says, and I give him a confused look. He shakes his head and looks at Master Pirate who chuckles. "She hasn't told you yet? Have you not guessed?"

"Who?" I ask, but I know; deep down, I think I've always known the identity of the true heir.

"Everleigh," Master Light says, and I turn around, walking out the cave as shock rolls through me.

* * *

"Everly?" I ask, opening the door to her rooms. I'm surprised when Tyrion walks out of a doorway to the left of the entry. He stops/pauses when he sees me, and the basket of clothes he was carrying drops to the floor. Tyrion hasn't changed much since when he was with the king's guards. He is still as handsome as I remember, with wavy brown hair and bright-blue eyes. He still looks and carries himself like a guard.

That hasn't changed, but I know his loyalty *has* changed. Maybe he knows who Everly is, and that's why he is here. He guards her. Maybe he always knew, even when she was just another prisoner in the king's games.

"Cassandra, it is good to see you again," he says, but I'm in no mood for pleasantries. I need to talk to my best friend and find out some answers. It's like everything is clicking into place, everything that I ignored for so long when I shouldn't have.

"Did I come to the wrong room? I'm looking for Everly?" I ask, but I'm pretty sure I have the right rooms.

"No, I share a place with her," he tells me, yet another thing Everly hasn't told me about. *Is she with Tyrion?* "Everly is in that room." Tyrion points to a room opposite the one he left.

"Thank you," I say, walking to the door. I don't knock, just walk in, and Everly looks up from where she sits, brushing her hair in the mirror. She puts the brush down as I shut the door, and smiles at me.

"I'm so happy you came to see me . . ." She drifts off when I cross my arms and glare at her.

"You are the future queen? The heir of land and sea? How could you not tell me?" I demand. She appears shocked for a second, before a cold look crosses over her face. She starts to say something, but I hold my hand up, cutting her off. "I would have protected you, never judged you! I thought we were best friends, sisters! And you have been lying to me!"

"I don't *have* to tell you anything, Cassy, but I did try. Your pirates just never gave me an opportunity. Don't be mad at me for something I can barely admit to myself, for something I do not want to be," she says, her voice cracking at the end of the sentence and she walks over to the bed. She sits down, dropping her face to her hands and starts to cry. Not a little cry, but a heart-wrenching cry, full of fear and anger. I recognise those kind of tears, the tears you can't stop. All the anger and shock I feel fades away as quickly as it came. I walk over, sit next to her, and pull her into my arms. I guess I didn't think about what it must be like for her, and my anger seems nothing in comparison to what kind of future she is meant to have. She was tortured in that castle, lost her mother there, and now she is supposed to rule the very world that has been so cruel to her. *Who would want that?*

"Tell me everything," I whisper, as she calms down some time later. She shakily nods, pulling back and wiping her eyes. I reach across the bed, and get some tissues from the side, handing them to her. She wipes her eyes and blows her nose as I wait for her to explain everything to me. I look her over, examining her beautiful features, and it finally hits me. Her blonde hair is so very unlike the dark hair of the royals we know, but her blue eyes, they are family. They look like Ryland's, and that's why they always looked familiar to me.

"Before my mother died, she told me everything. Things I had no idea about, and really didn't want to know," she says and clears her throat. So, she didn't know from the beginning about all of this. It hasn't been that long since she learned of her own past. When we grew up, I would never have guessed the girl I played board games and climbed trees with would be the future queen. Or that she was an heir to the crown. I guess that's why Onaya was the perfect place to hide her. Onaya is quiet, dead almost, and no one in the world would look for royalty there.

"My mother was the bastard child of a maid and the old king. The current queen is her half-sister, my aunt, and that makes Ryland and Hunter my cousins in a way," she says, and I squeeze her hand. When I marry Ryland and Hunter, we will be related in a way. I can't believe this whole time she was their cousin, and they never knew it. They think all their family is dead, or soon to be. I believe learning about Everly would help them. I think back to the ship, and the book I read that mentioned something about a fair-haired bastard child being born.

"I read a book that was on my pirates' ship, where it talked of there being a child born of a maid and the king . . .," I explain to her, and she hastily nods her head. When her fear-filled eyes look back at me, I know there is something more that she is scared to tell me.

"There's more," she says, holding back a sob. I can see she is scared I will reject her. Or that I will be frightened of her.

"Go on, I won't care what you are. You never cared that I'm a changed one, or that I could be dangerous. You protected me, just as I will protect you. What is in our blood, what we are born with, doesn't make the choices in our life for us. We get to choose, and you will choose your own path," I tell her firmly, and she sobs, wiping her eyes with the tissue.

"My mother said that one day, a mermaid man washed up on the shores of Onaya. She said she hid him in her home, that she looked after him as he suffered from poisoning of some sort," she smiles a little, "she said they fell in love with each other."

"Are you saying what I think you are?" I ask in disbelief.

"Yes, I'm half mermaid. But I don't have any powers or a tail," she points at her legs, making me laugh.

"No, but mermaids are said to be able to sing men to their deaths, and no man could resist their deadly beauty. Have you tried singing?" I ask, and she shakes her head.

"I haven't sung since I was a child. My mother always told me not to. Maybe there was a reason for it," she says quietly. It must be hard for her to know her mother kept so many secrets from her, even if it was for her own good. The sea god had to know who she was, and made sure that we grew up close together.

"So many secrets, so much hidden from us and planned out for our lives . . . are you going to be able to take the throne if I get it for you?" I ask the most important question. Now that I think about it, there isn't anyone else I could imagine giving the throne to. It has to be Everly, it always has been.

"I don't want it. I don't want the responsibility that will come with it, but I don't have a choice. I've accepted that," she says sadly.

"Sometimes in life, the things we don't want are

the best things for us," I tell her, and she rests her head on my shoulder. "I never wanted my mark, and I never wanted to go to the sea, but they were exactly what I needed."

"I would make a bad queen, and I have no idea what I'm doing. I may have the right blood, but that doesn't make a queen. It doesn't make a ruler," she replies, and hearing her say that, just makes me more certain that she is the right person for the job. A queen that wanted the throne, would kill for it, is not the right kind of queen that Calais needs to heal. Everly is thinking of the people, not the fame and riches. She may be young like I am, but she won't ever be alone when she takes the throne.

"I think you will make a brilliant queen, if that's anything. If I could give the throne to a person of my choosing, it would be you. You know why?" I ask, and she shakes her head.

"You are kind, yet firm when you need to be. You have suffered, but you have risen above the evil you have faced, and you are so strong. You can do this. You were born for this," I say, knowing every word is true.

"Cass, I'm no queen. I don't know a thing about ruling," she mutters as she lifts her head and pushes her hair behind her ear.

"Neither do I, but the master will help you. You can't do worse than the king has done, but promise me something?" I ask, and she gives me a questioning look. "Promise me your first law will be that changed ones are free. That anyone that hunts, kills, or sells them, will be hung for it," I ask.

"It will be my first law, and there will be many others. Changed ones, the world needs them, and we should protect them," she says.

"What do you mean?" I ask, curious.

"While I've been here, I've watched how the changed ones help Calais. They make the plants healthy, they make rain clouds, they give their magic to Calais. We need them. The world is dying because we keep killing them. Changed ones are a gift from the gods for the world, and we keep throwing the gift away rather than using it. We need a balance, or we will never know peace," she tells me, and I smile.

"Makes sense, there always has to be a balance, and our powers could help. Imagine if I used my water powers to water the trees and other plants in Onaya," I muse.

"A lot of people wouldn't be starving, that's for sure," she says, and then I remember what happened before I found out about her being the heir. We have big problems we need to sort.

"We have to leave, and go to the mermaids now," I tell her.

"Why?" she asks.

"Part of the deal I made with the sea god means I need to find a crown. It's with them," I tell her, and I know I need her with me. They might not attack us if Everly can be at my side and speak with me. She has their blood, and she is their people. When Everly meets my eyes, I know I don't have to tell her all that. She knows what I'm thinking.

"Then I'm at your side. I can fight really well, and I guess we should bring Tyrion with us. He is a brilliant fighter, too," she says, not mentioning the main reason she needs to come, but I know better than to push her on it. She has said she is at my side, much like I'm on hers always.

"Sure," I grin, and then nod my head at the door. "Are you and Tyrion together?"

"No, he is my best friend. I mean, I think he is as hot as anything, but he never has tried to take it further. I don't think he likes me that way, and I won't risk our friendship by trying to find out," she tells me, her eyes drifting to the door for a second. "He knows who I am, and I think he knows I will likely have no choice in who I marry. He won't get too close. Might be something I will have to get used to."

"He will give in, you are stunning and amazing, Everly. Plus, you shouldn't give up, he is pretty handsome," I grin.

"I won't tell your fiancés you said that," she laughs.

"You probably shouldn't, they would attempt to kill him," I say, and we both laugh.

"Everything is changing, and we are growing up," she says suddenly.

"Yes, but all things change. And this is for the better. We can do this together," I say, pulling her into a hug.

"Yes, we can, or at least we can try," she whispers.

"Will I have to call you queen? Or your highness?" I joke.

"No, never you. I'm always Ev or Everly to you," she laughs and squeezes me tight.

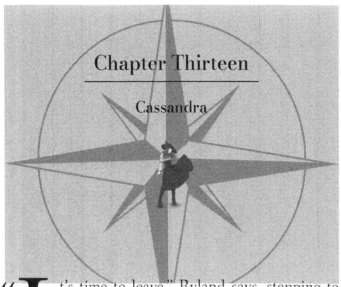

Chapter Thirteen

Cassandra

"I t's time to leave," Ryland says, stepping to my side as I rest my head on Vivo's nose. Vivo doesn't growl at my chosen, she is happy to let him near her, but no one else. In the last two days, while we have gotten the ship ready to leave and enough food to last us the trip, she has caused problems. It was like she could sense I had to leave, and I was distressed about it. It's not that I don't want to leave the mountains, because I do, but I don't want to leave Vivo. She feels like family to me.

"Vivo, I have to leave, and go to the mermaids. I can't take you with me, sorry, girl. I'm scared they might try to attack you," I say, and she huffs, snow falling on my feet as it drips from her mouth. "I know you want to come, but the mermaids might take offense to me flying a dragon to them. So, can you stay here with the mountain people until they leave, and go with them? We will meet at the other side." She huffs again, stepping back and flying off the mountain, the rush of air making me step back.

"I don't think that was a yes," Ryland says wryly, as he wraps his arms around my waist.

"It wasn't. She is stubborn, but she won't do anything that will risk my life. I know that," I say, watching her fly away towards the other dragons flying around outside.

"Like her rider," Ryland chuckles, and kisses my forehead. "We must leave if we have any chance of getting to the mermaids and back in time." I let Ryland lead me away from the landing dock and down towards the bottom of the mountains. People are rushing around us so much that they don't even notice me and Ryland. The mountains are in a panic trying get ready for the war. The announcement was made not long after I left Everly's room, and it's been crazy here ever since.

"Is the ship ready?" I ask.

"Yes, we had to move it the edge of the waterfall, but the crew have it all set up to go. We believe it will take two weeks to travel to the mermaids in the Lost Sea. The Lost Sea is extremely dangerous to travel, with a lot of jagged rocks and broken ships. It will be easier to navigate out of the Lost Sea than in, so only a week to travel from there to the king," Ryland explains to me.

"Do you think the mermaids will make a deal with us?" I ask him, wanting to know his opinion.

"No, not with us, but perhaps with you and Everly." I give him a confused look, "Mermaids are known to make deals with powerful women. They do not like men and usually kill them. I still have no idea how my father got close enough to make a deal with them," he says, and I hate the pain I see in his eyes when he speaks of his father.

"Do you know who Everly is to you?" I ask quietly.

"No, what do you mean? Should I?" he replies.

"She told me last night that she is the heir. She is your cousin, a bastard child born from your grandfather's affair with a maid," I tell him, and he wraps an arm around my waist, pulling me to his side. I look up to see a big smile on his lips.

"You have no idea how glad it makes me to learn she is the heir. I always felt . . . protective of her. Like she was my sister in a way. I know Hunter noticed it, too. Hunter and I never wanted the throne, and we would never have been good kings. Our father scarred us too much, and we want to be free more than we want to rule," he tells me as we walk through the cave, coming out to the bay full of ships. They are being moved, and now our ship is right at the edge of the waterfall, with people carrying boxes onto the ship.

"The sea god set a lot of this up, I know he did. He likely made you want to protect her. Everyone seems to want to protect Everly, but no one ever questioned why they felt that way. It's because she is the true queen," I say, looking up to see Dante and Everly talking on the ship. Dante grins when he sees me, walking away and to the edge of the plank of wood that leads to the ship. Ryland lets me go, so I can run up to Dante and wrap my arms around him.

"I haven't seen you much, I've missed you," I mumble.

"I had to train and every time I came to find you, you were busy," he complains. Before I can reply, he kisses me, sweeping me up into his arms with the passionate kiss.

"I won't go, I'm sorry. I won't do it . . . I just can't!" I hear Roger exclaim. Breaking away from the kiss, I turn to see him standing in the middle of the ship, shouting at Jacob.

"That's why I told you where we are going, Roger. You don't have to come," Jacob placates, holding his hands up. I'd forgotten that my pirates had rescued Roger from the mermaids. He must have such horrible memories and lingering fears of them. It would explain why he's so adamant in his refusal to come with us.

"The mermaids will kill you all, you fools!" Roger shouts, and storms over to me. Dante keeps me in his arms, and moves me slightly to the side, so he can defend me if needed.

"Please don't go, Miss Cassandra. They will kill you and everyone on this ship," Roger begs me, grabbing my hands.

"I have to, but I'm not a weak child, nor defenceless. Do not worry about me," I tell him and move away from Dante to pull Roger into a hug. I whisper quietly, so only he can hear me. "Don't fear your past, for you are better than that. Now go, have a good future, and we shall see you again one day." I pull away from the embrace, and he gives me a sharp nod before walking around me and Dante, heading off the ship.

"It was the right thing to tell him where we are

headed. He doesn't deserve to see the past he is still tormented by," I say to Jacob as he comes over to me.

"But you have to do just that, how is that fair?"

"It's life," I say sadly, leaning up and kissing his scarred cheek. I walk away from them and head to the very front of the ship. I climb up on the edge, seeing the mermaid statue underneath me and the waterfall right in front of me. I hear my pirates shouting orders, getting the ship ready to go, but I just keep my eyes on the water. Suddenly, I feel two hands slide around my waist.

"Ready, little bird?" Hunter asks me, resting his chin on my shoulder, and the ship moves, heading straight for open water. As we break through the waterfall, it splashes down on us, and I keep my eyes open as we move through to the other side. The ship turns sharply to the right, down a long passage of caves, and then we finally see the first rays of sunlight from outside.

"This is it, isn't it? We have to fight and win," I whisper as the daylight hits my face and warms my skin. The contrast of the cold sea winds with the warm light is soothing. It almost makes me feel free, like I can make my own choices and have the future I've always wanted.

"First, we need to convince one of the deadliest

races in this world to help us. A race known for killing first and never asking questions later," Hunter comments and turns my head, keeping his hand on my cheek. "But before any of that, I want my girl to kiss me." I smirk, before doing just as he asks.

Chapter Fourteen

Dante

"Cassandra?" I walk up to where she is sitting on the deck, staring up at the stars. The sea is quiet, and half the ship is sleeping while the other half keeps watch. I expected her to be sleeping, but here she is. She turns to look at me, the moonlight lighting up her beautiful face and framing every stunning feature. Her long brown hair moves around her in the wind as she stands up and walks over to me. I can't help myself; when she is close enough, I grab her hips and pull her to me, pressing my lips to hers. She lets out a little moan, and her small, soft hands dive into my hair.

"Dante," she whispers against my lips, pulling

back a little but not going far. "Why are you awake at this time of night?"

"I'm on watch tonight," I explain to her. "But why are *you* awake, pretty girl?" I ask.

"I couldn't sleep," she replies.

"The sea god?" I ask, knowing he used to invade her dreams a lot.

"Something like that," she says, putting on a brave face.

"Tell me, Cassandra. You don't need to hide anything from me," I say, rubbing circles on her back.

"It's a selfish thing, and I know we have bigger problems . . . so don't worry," she mumbles.

"What is it?"

"I want to marry you all, just in case, well, in case we lose this war," she admits, and I can't say I haven't had the same thoughts.

"Then we will get married on the ship. We only need the blessing of the gods, and I know we have that,"

"Can we do that?" She asks.

"If you don't mind not having a big dress, or pretty things. We can only offer you a ship and our vows."

"I only want you all, nothing else matters. I want

you all as my husbands if anything–" her voice catches, and I lift her head with my hand, forcing her to look into my eyes.

"I'm not going to lie to you and say we will win this for certain. I can't promise you that, and I won't ever lie to you. But I *do* know one thing for certain, you are mine, and my soul will never leave yours," I tell her, and a tear falls down her cheek as she stares up at me.

"I'm worried and scared, and I don't like to admit that to anyone. I try so hard not to be, but there is so much against us,"

"Being worried and scared means you are alive. It's normal, but use those emotions to keep yourself going. Or tell me, and I will help you," I tell her, and she nods, resting her head against my chest.

"What do mermaids look like?" she asks me, and my memories flash back to the three mermaids I saw once.

"Honestly? They have a beauty to them, but it's a deadly beauty that makes you want to go to them despite the danger. Their tails almost glow, and I know that they have the ability to change from tails to legs at will. I saw a mermaid transform to legs in what seemed like seconds." I explain.

"I need to tell you something, but don't tell anyone yet. She doesn't want everyone to know, and it's her secret to tell the world."

"Go on," I encourage her.

"Everly is half mermaid," she says, and I'm speechless for a few minutes, not knowing exactly what to say to that. Mermaids usually all have different coloured hair, and certainly are not blond. They typically have purple or blue hair. It's one of the easiest ways to differentiate their race. I know it's a good chance she got the blonde hair from her mother, and she clearly doesn't have any of the mermaids' abilities.

"I didn't expect you to say *that*, pretty girl," I finally say. "It might be a good thing, though. The mermaids might want a deal between the land and the sea. She is both."

"Everly could be the queen of both the land and the sea, it's her birthright. No mermaid queen or king is going to like her being on the throne," she says, and there is so much worry in her eyes. So much stress. It's all we have had recently, stress and fear.

"A worry for another day, another time. Come, I want to show you something," I say. She nods, letting me slide our hands together and lead us across the deck to the stairs. I let her go down first, and I follow her down the stairs. She waits for me at the bottom, and we walk towards my room. I open the door for her, leading her in and shutting it after. Cassandra sits on my bed, lighting a candle while I open my box and look through it.

"When I saw the mermaids while we were saving Roger, they had these necklaces on. They all wore them, and when they went from their mermaid tails to their legs, it would glow," I explain and pull out my notebook. I take it over to her, flipping through the pages until I get to the images of the mermaids I wanted to show her. Cassandra looks at every drawing with me, pausing on the necklace. It's a star shape, about the size of your thumb and filled with lines carved in the purple crystal.

"I think the necklaces are made with the same thing as your crystal stick. If I'm right, they will want it. It's clear it is something special to them," I tell her, and her whole face lights up. She puts the notebook next to me on the bed and climbs onto my lap. I groan when she starts kissing my neck, her teeth grazing over my pulse, as my hands slide down her back, holding her to me.

"I have to watch the ship, pretty girl,"

"Well, I say it's time you had a break, and I know just what we could do, pretty boy," she grins in the most seductive way possible, and I know no man could ever deny her.

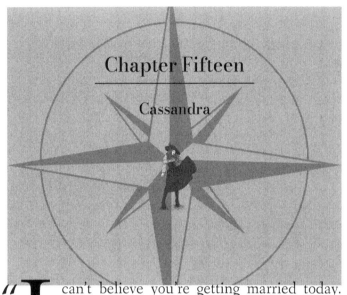

Chapter Fifteen

Cassandra

"I can't believe you're getting married today. My best friend is getting married," Everly exclaims, plaiting another part of my hair, and pulling it up into the bun she has made up. I stare at myself in the mirror, barely recognising my own reflection. I'm no longer the young girl that left Onaya. The one who was innocent and didn't know a thing of the world. I'm no longer that lonely girl, and I know I will never be alone again.

"It will happen for you one day. A guy is going to come into your life and knock you off your feet," I say, knowing I'm right.

"That will–" Everly's voice drifts off as the sea god's desperate voice over takes hers in my mind.

"The king knows where you are going; he knows

everything. You must hurry! You must get my crowns, and return them to me with the king's soul." I gasp, falling off the chair as he leaves my mind.

"Cassy," Everly picks me up, giving me a concerned look.

"The sea god says the king knows what we are doing. How is that possible?" I ask her, and she shakes her head.

"I have no idea, but don't let him ruin this special day for you. Forget what he said, and move past it," she tells me, and there is a knock at the door. I stand up as Everly opens it slightly.

"We need to speak to Cassandra. Alone," Ryland insists. Everly looks back at me for confirmation, and I nod my assent.

"I will go check to make sure everything is ready," Everly says, widening the door, so she can walk out. Ryland comes in, holding a long red dress. Everly's eyes stay on the dress, just as mine do, until she grins widely at me and shuts the door.

"It's beautiful," I breathe out as I step closer. Ryland hooks the dress on the back of the door. It's tight at the top, with red crystals all on the sides, and they go down the dress as it flows out. It's a dress meant for a queen.

"Laura stole this from the castle when we left,

and she told me to give it you a few months ago. She said she wore this dress at her wedding, and my mother wore it at hers. It's one of the only family traditions I want to keep. Would you please wear it today?" he asks me, the vulnerability in his voice makes me wrap my arms around him.

"It would be my honour to wear it. We will keep it to give to our children as well," I say, and he lifts my head with his hand.

"When did I get so lucky to have you? To be marrying you today?" he asks, and I shake my head.

"No, I'm the lucky one. I'm so, so lucky to have fallen into the sea and to have gotten rescued by pirates," I chuckle, and he kisses me. I moan as he picks me up, pushing me against the wall by the door as I hold onto him, and he deepens the kiss. I move away from his lips, trailing my lips down his neck, feeling his pulse beating against my lips.

"Cassandra, we have a wedding to get to," he groans, and a bang at the door makes us jump apart.

"I'm back, but I don't want to see any naked bits. Is it safe to come in?" Everly shouts, and Ryland laughs low as I step away.

"It's safe to come in. I was just leaving," he replies and steps around me, opening the door and letting Everly in.

"I'm going to clean up for the wedding. See you in a short while," Ryland tells me tenderly, and walks out the door. Everly shuts it, her hands going to the dress and lifting it off the back of the door.

"This is an amazing dress, look at all those crystals. The fabric, and well, everything. It must have cost a small fortune,"

"It's Ryland and Hunter's family tradition. The royals wear this dress when they get married,"

"It is fitting for a queen. I guess I might have a dress one day," Everly says, but her voice is full of fear instead of hope or longing. She still doesn't want the crown, and I don't know if I can blame her. I go to say something, trying to think of anything to make it easier for her. She cuts me off with a harsh shake of her head.

"I know my future, and I accept it. It doesn't mean I'm not fearful of it. Now give me a reason to smile, and let's get you married," she asserts. I laugh, pulling my clothes off until I'm in only my underwear. Everly helps me step into the dress and then does the laces up on the back. It takes a while, and when it's finally done, I step over to the mirror.

"You look like a queen," Everly comments, and she isn't wrong. The red dress makes me look less like someone I recognise and more like a royal, which

I'm not. Well, I guess I will be, temporarily, when I marry Ryland and Hunter, because they are princes. Honestly, although the dress is stunning, I miss my normal clothes. They are more comfortable and feel like home. I hear the distant noise of sweet sounding music, and Everly grabs my hand.

"It's time. I hope for nothing more than a beautiful future for you. A free one," she says, kissing my cheek before opening the door for me. I have to wipe away a few tears before I can respond.

"I want the same for you. Thank you for being here. I wish it was my father walking me down the aisle, but I doubt he would have," I say, looking at the door and pulling the handle to open it. The music gets louder, and I realise someone is playing a guitar.

"He would have. Your father would have done anything for you, even if he didn't always show it. In the dungeons, he told me that putting his child first is the best thing you can ever do. He loved you wholeheartedly. He might not be here in person, but I would bet his soul is watching today, just like your mother's," Everly says, and hooks her arm into mine.

"I hope they are, too," is all I can say as I walk out the room and towards the stairs. I walk up first, coming out onto the deck. Someone has lit dozens of little candles, and they are lined all over the floor.

There are lanterns hanging from ropes that lead to the middle of the ship, where my pirates are all standing waiting for me. Tyrion stands in the middle of them a little further back. I can't take my eyes off them to appreciate the decorations, because they all look so perfect to me. My bond with them flares to life, taking over as I feel how much they love and desire me. I know they would do anything for me right now. I walk over to them, wiping more tears away as I get to the middle of them. They hold hands with each other, and I slide my hands into Ryland's and Chaz's hands, since they are next to me.

"No tears today, little bird," Hunter murmurs, his dark eyes watching me from the other side of the circle.

"They are happy tears, I promise," I whisper. Tyrion's loud voice comes from behind us, and the music cuts off.

"We all gather here today to witness the marriage of Cassandra of Onaya and her chosen. The gods tell us life is eternal, that there is no end, even in death. When two souls are bonded, they become eternal together. There is no end for them either. We ask the gods for their blessing, for their strength, and for this marriage to be blessed in their light and love. If you have anything you wish to say, now is the time."

I clear my throat, gaining all of their attention, even though I doubt I ever lost their attention for even a moment. "I read in a book once, that the meaning to life is love. Now when I read it, I remember thinking that was stupid and untrue. That there was no way that love could be everything in life. I was wrong. I will admit, when we first met, I didn't think there was a chance in hell I would fall for any of you pirates," I say, and they all chuckle.

"Did you decide that when you tried to jump off the moving ship, or when you hit Chaz over the head with the book?" Jacob asks, and I roll my eyes.

"Let me finish." I chuckle when they nod their heads, almost in unison with each other. "But I did fall for you, one by one. When we were separated, and I knew I never wanted to be away from any of you again. Love is just a simple word. It doesn't describe how we feel, how unimaginable it is to feel this way for another person. So, I can't put into words how I feel for each one of you, but I know you can feel it. Like I can feel how much you each love me." I stop, unable to go on more. Ryland kisses my cheek, while Chaz squeezes my hand. Every one of my pirates look close to breaking the circle and kissing me, telling me how they feel without words. Our bond tells me enough.

"The marriage of Cassandra and her chosen has begun," Tyrion says, and walks into the circle, with Jacob and Hunter parting to let him in. Tyrion looks at me as he pulls a thin needle out of his pocket and a pot of black ink.

"We discussed the fact that we don't have six rings, and Zack suggested a mark on all your ring fingers would be better? It's a tradition in Sixa, but you have final say."

"You would do that for me?" I ask, glancing around at them all.

"We are already marked as yours, this would just make you our legal wife. Yes, we all want this,"

"Can I have the same mark?" I ask.

"If you wish," Tyrion says, and I pull my hand from Chaz's to hold it out.

"Just above the ring please," I ask, and he nods, dipping the needle into the ink and drawing onto my finger. It hurts as he cuts, but I keep my eyes on each one of my pirates one after the other. When it's done, I look down at the hexagon, and the tiny triangle mark in the middle.

"Six lines make the hexagon, one line for each of us, and you are our centre," Ryland explains as he holds his hand out, and Tyrion starts cutting his finger.

"I love you all," I say quietly, but I know they hear me. When Tyrion has marked all the guys, he smiles at us.

"Now you are married, congratulations," he says, seconds before he's pushed out of the way, and my six husbands pull me into an embrace.

Chapter Sixteen

Cassandra

"Being sick, *again?*" Everly asks me as I throw up into the bucket by the bed. I look up to see her close the door behind her. I wait until I don't feel like I will throw anything else up before I answer her.

"It's seasickness, I guess. Chaz says some people get it," I answer, picking up a towel and wiping my mouth from the awful taste. I pick up the glass of water off the side and look up at Everly, who leans against the door. She waits for me to drink it and then to take the bucket to the bathroom to empty it.

"There is something else it could be," she says slowly when I walk back into the room.

"Like what?" I ask.

"I forget just how shielded you were sometimes," Everly chuckles, "no wonder you haven't thought about it."

"About what?" I demand, wanting to know what she thinks. Chaz suggested all sorts of things to help with the seasickness, but nothing has worked.

"On Onaya, when the women were in the earliest stage of pregnancy, they sometimes would be sick every morning," she says quietly, but I move back on the bed, shock rolling through me. I never thought about it, about the chances of getting pregnant. I guess in the back of my head I knew we weren't being safe, but it's still so shocking.

"But no one ever gets pregnant. It's so rare in younger women, that I didn't think it could happen so quickly," I say in a rush.

"That was on Onaya, where the women were starved, and they weren't strong enough to get pregnant. You have been well fed and looked after. It's not surprising to me at all. I just assumed you would have thought about it," she explains.

"Well, I didn't," I bite out and take a deep breath. "Sorry, I'm not mad with you, but at myself. This baby couldn't have come at a worse time."

"You do have a lot of husbands, Cassy," she says

with a laugh, but I'm in a daze. I can't even think about anything other than the fact we are heading into mermaid waters in less than four hours, and I could be pregnant. I could be carrying a baby. My baby. My eyes water as I look down at my flat stomach, where my hands have instinctively gone to cradle.

"The baby could be a royal," she says suddenly, and it starts to dawn on me that my baby could be another heir.

"No one could prove that. Like you said, I have six husbands. The baby could be any one of theirs," I admit to her, and she shakes her head, both of us silent for a long time. This changes so much, but I can't help the sudden wave of protectiveness and happiness I feel at the idea of having a baby. If we win, my baby would be born into a world in peace. With six overprotective dads to watch her. Not that I know it's a girl, but for some reason a little girl with brown hair and a cheeky grin pops into my mind.

"You cannot tell anyone," I suddenly shout out. Everly gives me a worried look as she comes and sits on the bed next to me. She reaches over and grabs my hand.

"Your pirates would be overjoyed. I don't understand why you want to keep the baby a secret," Everly says, confusion written all over her face.

"Possible baby, I might just be sea sick," I mutter, and she shakes her head at me. She looks about as convinced of that as I am.

"No, I'm almost certain you're pregnant. I can tell there is something different about you, a glow, and it's been there for weeks," she says, earnestly.

"I could sense a change. I have always been able to see more than the average person. All people have this glow about them, but yours was always more. I never told you, because being different was so dangerous back then. It still is, in a way. Your glow was a bright blue colour, with white spots. Now, it's white with a blue line around it," she tells me, looking out the window and towards the sea. Maybe she does have some kind of gifts from her mermaid side after all.

"They would *never* let me fight the king if they knew. They would never let me near the mermaids. My pirates would turn this ship around and hide me to keep me safe, and I can't let that happen. If I am pregnant, then I want a world my baby can be safe in, and so I can't hide," I tell her, holding my hand over my stomach, and she nods her agreement.

"As complicated as it is, I understand why you don't want to tell them, but you have to know I won't leave your side," she says, and I smile.

"I know that," I say. A loud, drill-like noise screams through the room, and I scream as I hold my ears. Everly doesn't hold her ears, she just stands up and looks down at me, her blue eyes glowing a violet colour.

"Ev, what is it?" I manage to spit out, lying on my side as the noise gets louder, and then it suddenly cuts off. I gasp, trying to catch my breath as my ears ring. I sit up, and look over at Everly. She is just standing there, her eyes still glowing.

"Cass!" Jacob shouts, just before the door bursts open, and he rushes in. He stares at Everly for a split second, before rushing to me and helping me up off the bed.

"What the hell was that?" I ask him, and he shakes his head.

"No idea. What is wrong with your friend?" he asks me. I step up to Everly, putting my hands on her face.

"Ev?" I ask, but she doesn't respond. "Forgive me for this." I lift my hand, slapping her hard across the face, and she falls to the floor. I drop next to her, rolling her onto her back. She blinks up me and holds a hand to her face.

"You slapped me," she exclaims in shock.

"Your eyes were glowing, and I had to snap you out of it. I'm not going to say sorry for it," I respond, and Jacob chuckles as I stand up. Everly gets up with my help.

"Weapons, something is coming, and we need to be on deck," Jacob says, handing me a dagger. I accept it as Everly runs out of the room.

"Stand close to one of us," Jacob warns, and I grab his arm before he makes a move to step out of the room. I slide the dagger into his hand, and he shakes his head at me.

"I don't need a weapon; you forget who I am. I may be your wife now, but I do not need defending," I tell him, and he smiles, folding his hand over mine holding the dagger.

"You never know when you might need this, so please carry it. For me?" he asks me. I stare into his eyes for a moment, realizing he needs me to carry it for his own peace of mind. So for my pirate, I nod and slide the dagger into the side of my trousers.

"On deck, now!" I hear Everly shout loudly, and the sound of swords crashing together fills my ears. Jacob runs ahead of me, and I quickly follow. We run up the steps and out on to the deck just as a large scaly animal of some sorts jumps out of the water, heading straight towards us. It opens its mouth, and thousands of sharp teeth appear as the skin pulls back. Jacob swings his sword off his back, cutting it in half before it gets near us. I look around the deck, seeing dozens of the creatures in bits on the floor, my husbands are fighting them off, with some of the others helping. Everly jumps into the air in the middle of the ship, swinging around a small, thin sword and killing three of the creatures.

"I have an idea, get everyone in the middle of the ship," I shout to Jacob, who nods, trusting me. We run to the centre of the ship as Jacob shouts for everyone to follow us.

"You best have a good idea, little bird," Hunter says as he is the final one to get into position, joining us in the middle of the deck. I don't reply, I simply sit on the floor and close my eyes. When I feel everyone's energies surrounding me, I pray to the sea god they are close enough and that this works.

"Cass?" I hear Jacob question as I feel for my bond, and call my power. I open my eyes, and I imagine the water spreading all around us, creating a wall of water. It works, and the creatures bounce against it. I stand up, and the water keeps moving slowly around in circles. The creatures don't stop rushing against the wall of water, but they can't get in. Eventually, they seem to stop. Maybe they are just going to wait us out.

"Impressive," Tyrion comments, and Chaz places a hand around my waist.

"She certainly is," Chaz replies, smiling down at me and pressing his lips against mine for just a second.

"How close are we to the mermaids?" I ask as I remember where we are, and that I can't get lost in Chaz's lips right now.

"I think we are about to find out," Dante comments, pointing to the three outlines of people that appear on the other side of the water to our left. I step forward, with Ryland and Chaz keeping close to my side.

"Who are you?" I shout, as a hand presses into the water.

A sweet voice replies almost instantly. "The guards of the mermaids, and our king wishes you all to be killed." I look over at Hunter as he presses the crystal stick into my hand.

"I promised you I would keep it safe," he says firmly. I take it in my hand, and drop the water barrier between us quickly. The three people standing right in front of us are stunning, there is no other word to accurately describe them. They all have long blue hair, even the one male's hair is as long as the two females'. Their glowing blue eyes watch me, not one of them look away or even blink. They are completely naked; no clothes cover any part of their bodies, and it's awkward to look at. I hold the stick in the air, looking at the star necklaces that look like the same kind of crystal. Dante was right.

"I have something to trade with the king. I wish to see him," I say, and the mermaid man hisses.

"The king does not see a land child," he spits out.

"I am a changed one, not just a land child, and I demand he meets with me," I say, keeping my voice firm, but I know I haven't got a chance of convincing them when they look at me. One of the mermaid women laughs, just as Everly steps to my side. I look over to her as she stands tall and speaks loudly.

"I am the heir to the crown of the land, and I have mermaid blood as well. Do you not think your king would wish to meet me?" Everly challenges them. The mermaids all look between each other, before the mermaid in the middle presses her finger to her star necklace.

"Gyd liht aunns, fttaao kwnwe geffelln," the

mermaid says, keeping her blue glowing eyes on Everly as she speaks. I look over at Hunter, who is watching us closely, his hand wrapped around a red sword at his side. I know he will kill them if they don't let us see the king. We have too much to lose.

"The king will see the heir and the changed one. No one else is permitted into Merida, or they will be killed," the mermaid girl says and bows her head. "My name is Kiaw, and I have been told to personally promise your safety."

"If you think your king has chosen the weak ones to see him, he couldn't be more wrong," Ryland growls out, and turns me to face him. My pirates all surround me in a circle.

"Pretty girl, this is dangerous, and I don't want you to go," Dante says first.

"The world is dangerous, and we need that crown. There isn't a choice here, and I will be safe. Everly and I can fight our way out if we need to," I reply.

"We had to fall for a stubborn one, didn't we?" Jacob says to Chaz, who grins.

"Don't back down, but be respectful. Whoever this king is, he is clearly well respected," Ryland instructs, and I nod as Everly comes into our circle.

"I will protect her, but I don't think we are in any

danger. The king wants to meet us and make a trade," she says, and I grin.

"We will be in the water, and I kind of have a thing for it," I joke, making her chuckle.

"Good luck, and come back to us. We can't do anything, be anything, without you by our sides," Zack is the one that speaks the words I know they are all thinking. He steps closer, kissing my forehead, and then steps back. I turn around, walking straight up to the mermaids with Everly standing tall at my side.

"Let's go," I say, and the mermaid bows her head. The other two run off the ship, jumping into the air, and a warm glow appears around their legs as their legs turn into blue tails.

"How can we breathe underwater?" I ask Kiaw, who is left with us.

"A secret, one you will soon learn. Speak of it, and the sea will take your tongue," she warns with a hiss.

"We understand," Everly says, and there's a loud horn noise. We follow Kiaw over to the edge of the ship, where three water dragons come out of the water, flying and hovering back just next to the ship.

"The Dgaan will take you to our city, where we have places where you will be able to breathe, and there are many spots we can stop on the way to ensure you do not pass out," Kiaw explains and jumps off the ship, landing on the back of one the dragons.

"See you soon," I turn and say to my pirates, before running and jumping off the ship.

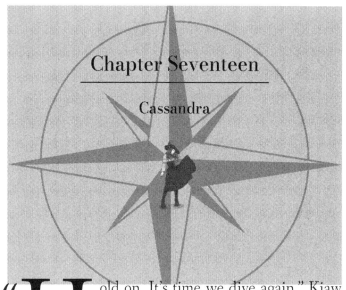

Chapter Seventeen

Cassandra

"Hold on. It's time we dive again," Kiaw says as I still gasp for breath in the small cave we have surfaced in. We have stopped in five caves as we travel deeper and deeper into the sea. It's become more and more painful at every stop, the pressure from the water feels like it's crushing me. Everly meets my eyes over the dragons we ride, but she doesn't look like she is having as much trouble as I am. It takes me a second to realise that it's because being under the sea is part of who she is.

"Ready," I shout, and the dragon dives under the water, swimming straight out of the cave while I hold onto her spikes and keep my eyes closed. When I see a light instead of only darkness in front of my eyes, I force them open in the cold, salty water. The sight before me is worth the slight sting. There's a town full of castle shaped buildings, some parts have a bubble surrounding them, and others are fully in the water. At the top of the tallest point, is a star. The half blue and half purple star is massive, and it lights up everything for miles. There are a lot of little white lights in the castles too, but I don't think they need them. Thousands of mermaids and different fish swim around the structures submerged in the water, before going into the bubble areas where their legs appear. Thank the gods they have fabric covering the parts of them that I'd rather not see, but they still don't seem to like to wear much. I look over at Everly, who appears as shocked as I feel. The dragons zoom towards the bubble, just as I start struggling for air, and they fly straight into it. The air hits my lungs, making me gasp and hold my chest, as my other hand holds onto the dragon. The dragons fly us straight through the city, where the mermaids with their multi-coloured hair all stop to watch us. I try not to stare at them, instead looking ahead at the biggest of the castles, which we are heading straight towards.

"Dmamma," Kiaw shouts, and the dragons dive towards the castle, landing on a long strip of stone that leads to massive glass doors. The pathway has a circular landing spot, which we are on, and a line of guards standing at the sides, holding long spears with what looks to be giant, deadly-looking forks on the end of them. I glance over at Everly as I slide off the dragon and see her push her wet, blonde hair over her shoulder, looking at the doors in front of us. I shake my own hair when I get off the dragon, looking down at my soaked clothes and already feel like I'm freezing down here.

"This way," Kiaw says succinctly, as I get to where she is standing in the middle of the path, and Everly walks to my side.

"A whole city underwater, it's amazing," Everly comments as we follow Kiaw down the path. I find myself examining the guards standing outside the doors. Still as statues, they remain motionless, not even blinking. I turn back and see Kiaw staring at me, but she looks away as she begins to speak.

"They are Merida guards, controlled by a mental connection to our king. We are all connected in Merida," she explains, even though I never asked. All I can think about is how creepy that is. Why would you need a connection like that to a whole army? Maybe that's how the king keeps his rule.

"I heard there was a queen, but yet we are seeing a king," Everly inquires.

"Queen Idia died a month ago, and her youngest son, King Damien, has taken the throne," she replies sadly. It's clear she cared deeply for the queen.

"Youngest? Don't the oldest usually take the throne?" I ask, and Kiaw stops right outside the doors, resting her hand on the handle to the right door.

"Yes, but here we believe in strength and blood. Blood wins the throne, and King Damien killed his two brothers to win," she says, her eyes narrowing on me. "Remember that he killed his family to claim his throne. He is not a mermaid to play games with." With that she pushes the door open, and we follow her through into the large room on the other side. The room has a large open window on the one side, stone floors, and burners that have a nice-smelling blue smoke coming out of them. There is a man standing silently in the middle of the room, his blue cloak and blue crystal crown on his head of blonde hair is all we can see from this distance.

"Leave us," the man's deep and frightening sounding voice says. Kiaw bows at his back, before running out of the room and leaving us alone. The man, the king, finally turns around and walks closer to us, but his eyes stay on Everly the whole time. When he steps closer, I can see the blue star on his forehead that matches his outfit. His purple eyes glow slightly as he stands still, watching and waiting.

"King Damien, I presume?" I say, and the king finally takes his eyes off Everly to look at me.

"Changed ones are not welcome in my sea. We do not respect your god here," he says simply, and turns his eyes back to Everly. I stay still as the king starts walking around us, slowly, and his eyes roll over Everly who doesn't move.

"I do not recognise your blood. Who is your father?" he asks.

"I don't know, and that is not something we came to discuss." Everly snaps.

"It may be the only thing I wish to discuss," he counters, and Everly swings around, walking straight up to the king before I can stop her.

"War is coming to the land, and when we win, I will rule. How long do you think it will be before war comes to the sea if we lose?" she says, her voice calculating, and the king laughs.

"What is your name?" he asks.

"Everleigh of Onaya," she replies, using her full name that I'm not used to hearing.

"You are not of Onaya," he says sharply as he watches her. There's something happening between them, and I almost don't want to interrupt, but I know I have to.

"We came to make a deal, a deal for this," I slide the crystal stick out of my trouser pocket and hold it up. The king looks at it, and then quickly back at Everly.

"You want the crown, the crown my mother swore to protect," he muses.

"Yes," I reply as Everly seems to have suddenly gone silent.

"I do not want the crystal," the king says, and all my hope disappears in a single moment.

"Then what do you want in exchange for the crown?" Everly demands, her hands going to her hips. The king steps closer to her, lifting a stray piece of her hair in his fingers. "King or not, I will cut your fingers off if you don't let go of my hair." she threatens him so smoothly that it catches him off guard for a second. I watch how his eyes slightly glow as she threatens him, and he takes a step back, placing his hands behind his back. Everly walks to my side, keeping her eyes locked on the king the whole time, and her hand on the sword at her hip.

"I will give you the crown, for a promise," the king finally says.

"What kind of promise?" I inquire, and the king laughs.

"Not a promise from you, changed one. No, a promise from the future queen," he says, and Everly crosses her arms.

"What do you want?" she asks in a not so nice manner. *There goes being respectful.*

"Your hand in marriage. Three months after you are crowned, you will come here and marry me. You will go through the ceremony of Merida and receive your bond to your race. We will rule both land and sea as one," he says, the somber look on his face lets me know he is deadly serious about marrying her. I glance at Everly, who meets my eyes and finally drops her eyes to my stomach, and I know her decision is made. She blurts out her answer before I can stop or reason with her.

"I accept your proposal, in exchange for the crown," as she says the words, his eyes light up bright blue, glowing like the star on his forehead does.

"Then, my future wife, I shall return," he says, smiling like the cat that finally got the bird he had always been hunting. I watch as he walks to the left, and a small door opens as he walks out. I wait for the door to close before attempting to say anything, but Everly immediately cuts me off.

"Don't, don't say it," she warns.

"We could have figured something else out, Ev," I whisper harshly, but she shakes her head.

"I knew what he wanted from the moment I walked into this room. I don't know how to explain it, but I knew," she says, confusing me.

"What are we going to do?" I ask, knowing I won't let my friend marry a stranger. A king who killed his own family for a throne.

"We are going to win the war. I am going to take my throne, my birthright and anything else, I will deal with. This isn't your promise, it is mine, and I will pay the price," she says and turns away from me before I can reply. We wait in silence until the king returns, walking in the room with an old, rusty box.

"The land king kept this with my mother to safeguard. He stole something of hers to force her to keep it safe," the king tells us, his eyes drifting back to the crystal stick. "The crystal is part of our power, and the mermaids believe it is sacred."

"You do not?" I ask, because I'm not sure I understand why he didn't wish to trade the crown for the crystal.

"I do, but there are better prizes to trade for," his eyes drift to Everly as he speaks, and she all but growls at him.

"Time to trade."

"Not yet. The box is enchanted. It needs royal blood from both land and sea in order to open it," he explains. He hands the box to me, which is heavier than I thought it would be, and pulls a blue dagger out of his cloak. King Damien cuts his hand quickly and holds the dagger out to Everly. She snatches it from him, slicing her own palm and placing it on the box. The second King Damien places his hand over Everly's, there is a clicking noise as the box unlocks. They both pull their hands away, and Everly opens the box, reaching in and pulling out the crown. I feel its power almost instantly, it rolls over me, and the urge to touch the crown is indescribable. Everly closes the box as she holds the crown, and I place the box on the floor.

"It belongs to a changed one," Everly says, offering me the crown when I look at her. The crown has a big white crystal in the middle, so clear that I can see my reflection in it.

"No, it belongs to the sea god, but we will borrow it for now," I say and place my hands on the crown, feeling its power rush through me. My bond with my pirates bursts to life, and it's like I can feel them right next to me. Their worry, their love, all of their emotions, and it soothes me.

"You should only touch it when you truly need to. Believe me, I know the power of a god's gifts," King Damien suggests, and I open my eyes to see him offering me a small woven bag. Despite feeling that I don't want to let go of the crown, I force myself to put the crown in the bag, and then I tie the bag on my back.

"We must leave now," I say, and pull the crystal stick out of my pocket, handing it to the king. "Think of it as a goodwill gift from the land." The king nods, accepting the crystal stick, and he turns to Everly, offering her it.

"It will protect you, you should take it," he suggests, and she smiles in an overly sweet way, before picking the stick up and throwing it across the room where it bounces off the wall.

"You may have my promise to marry you, but no gifts or tricks will ever get you my heart or my affection," she spits out, before storming around the king as he laughs.

"We shall see, my queen."

"Your queen is all I will ever be," she says and opens the door, waiting for me to follow her. We walk out, the sound of the king's deep laugh follows us, even through the closed door.

Chapter Eighteen

Cassandra

"Cassandra is back!" I hear someone yell loudly, but the water in my ears makes it impossible for me to know who shouted. I stroke the dragon who brought me to the surface and slide off its back, falling into the cold water. I see Everly do the same thing, catching up to swim right next to me. Kiaw left us when we were near the surface, not even waving goodbye at us. I can't stop thinking about the promise Everly made, and trying to figure out how she is going to get out of it. She can't end up married to man she clearly doesn't like. I look up as I get near the ship, seeing the rope ladder just before it's thrown right in front of me in the water. I swim to it, grabbing hold and climbing up. When I get near the top, hands pull me up the rest of the way, and I'm pressed against a familiar-smelling chest.

"You're back," Jacob whispers against my wet hair, soothing a hand down my back. I feel a towel wrap around me, and Jacob rubs his big hands up and down my back to dry me off. I really do need to get out of these freezing cold clothes, but I'm comfortable in Jacob's warm embrace.

"Did you ever doubt I would come back?" I ask as I pull away a little, and see Tyrion pulling Everly onto the deck. She looks far better than I thought she would considering she just agreed to marry a mermaid king.

"Cassandra?" I hear Chaz shout, and I pull away from Jacob to see him, Ryland, Hunter, and Dante running over. They each hug me, some kissing me gently, and it makes me instantly relax for the first time since we got here.

"Good to see you're back safely. Did you get the crown?" Ryland asks me, and I nod, pulling the bag off my back and holding it up. I don't want to take it out of the bag. It isn't worth the power rush at the moment, but they don't seem to question me when I put the bag back on my back.

"What did the king want?" Hunter asks, his voice

is cold. I look at Everly, seeing Tyrion stroking her arms, but she is already looking back at me. She shakes her head once, and I know that she doesn't want me to say anything. I can't blame her, but everyone will find out eventually. Still, it isn't my secret to tell.

"Nothing that cost me anything," I say honestly, and they all look between me and Everly.

"Should we worry, pretty girl?" Dante asks.

"No, trust me," I insist, and none of them say a word for a second.

"We need to turn this ship around, and head for the castle. Time to leave," Ryland shouts the end part, and everyone moves away except for him.

"We trust you, end of story. Now Zack is in the kitchens, and your stomach keeps rumbling. Go eat something," he says and kisses my forehead before going to help Dante with some ropes. I smile at them all, watching them running around and organising everything for us to leave. I walk straight to my room first, pulling my wet clothes off and changing into some spare ones. I plait my hair after squeezing some of the water out of it. I hold the bag close to me as I walk down the stairs and towards the kitchens, hearing a shout. I run forward, stopping at the sight of Zack holding a small, pink kitten. He looks over at me, and raises his spare hand to beckon me over with a big smile.

"I heard Salty Sam in the barrels again, so I went to look to try to get him out. The little bugger scratched me when I opened the barrel," he says, placing the kitten back in the barrel when I get to his side. I look down inside the barrel to see Salty Sam, with two little pink kittens snuggled up to her side.

"I thought Salty Sam was a boy," I say in shock, and Zack laughs.

"As did we all, but she never let us close enough to actually find out. Now we know, and there are two more mouths to feed," he says with a grin.

"I'm sure we will find them a home with a family somewhere, after everything is over," I say, placing the bag on one of the other barrels. Zack pulls me into his arms, holding me close against him as his fingers rub circles on my back.

"How did it go?" he asks after we just stand there holding each other a while, with the small kittens making tiny meows.

"Better than expected, and we have the crown," I say, and my stomach takes that moment to rumble loudly, causing Zack to laugh.

"Let's get some food in you," he says, pulling away and walking over to another barrel.

"Zack?" I call quietly.

"Yes," he replies as he pulls a loaf of bread out.

"I love you," I say, and he stops, looking me in the eye.

"I love you, Cassandra. I always have, and I always will," he tells me and starts cooking. I watch him silently, just taking in how he cuts the food up and moves about the kitchen/galley. He knows exactly what he is doing.

"So, what are you making? Can I help?" I ask.

"No, you can rest, and let your husband take care of you," he tells me, and I laugh, letting him do just that. When he brings me a tray with bread cut up, a bowl of something hot that smells amazing, and an apple, it nearly brings me to tears as I realise I could lose all of this. This normality, this caring, messed up pirate who I love. Everything could be gone because of the war, and I was stupid to think we might get out of this alive.

"Hey, don't cry," Zack's leather-covered hand wipes a tear away as I stare at him. "What was that for?" he asks me, still keeping his hand on my cheek.

"I'm happy, and I love this normal, ordinary moment between us. I'm scared it could all be taken from me in a few weeks," I admit to him.

"Nothing will be taken from us. We will make sure of that," he says firmly.

"How can we make sure of it? I have to fight the king, and he is so powerful. Until now, I didn't really think of what I would have to do," I say quietly.

"Are you scared of him? Or scared of losing everything more?" he asks me.

"Everything . . . I'm not scared of him," I say firmly, but my voice doesn't come out as confident as I wanted it to.

"It's normal to be scared," he tells me.

"I know," is all I can whisper back.

"You won't be alone, you know that, right? The king will fall at your hand, but we will be at your side as it happens," he tells me, and I wish it was as easy as his words make it sound. *We are going to war, and I'm scared what the price might be for us all.*

Chapter Nineteen

Cassandra

"**R**yland!" I moan out his name as I collapse on his chest, both of us breathing heavily. As we calm down, he slides out of me. He kisses my forehead, before rolling us over and leaning over me with a big smile.

"That was a nice wake up call, after you snuck out of bed earlier," he comments gruffly.

"I thought you were sleeping," I say. I didn't want him to know I was sick again, or let him see me that way, so I snuck out of the room and used an empty bathroom.

"Yes, but my body knows when you aren't next to me, even in sleep," he says, lifting his hand and pushing a piece of hair off my face. "You look tired."

"I can't sleep well, not with everything we know

is going to happen soon," I admit to him, and he kisses me. Just a brief, sweet kiss.

"I will hold you until you fall asleep," he says, but it's a demand hidden in a chiding tone. "No one, or no future, will hurt you when you're in my arms." His words have the desired effect, and as he lies down next to me, holding me close, I drift off into a peaceful sleep.

"Cassandra, it has been a while," the sea god's voice fills my mind, just as I open my eyes to see I'm standing in his cave. I look up at the hole in the cave, the sight of the Storm Sea above, and finally back down to the Sea God who sits on a chair in the middle of the cave, not far from me.

"Why is the Storm Sea the way it is? So dangerous and angry?" I inquire, looking back up at it.

"The Storm Sea was where I was born, and I have a higher connection to it. My emotions control the sea," he explains to me, and it makes sense why the sea is so angry now.

"Change is coming," I tell him, and he nods, looking up at the hole where we can see the sea churning.

"You could be so much more, Cassandra, but I see now that the powers of a god were never meant for you," he says.

"Is that what you tried to offer me once before?" I ask.

"Yes, only you chose love. Gods cannot love; it is a curse we all must bear," he tells me.

"Why am I here?" I ask.

"I do not want to send you to war, to risk losing your soul. I know what you must do in order to win, do you? You must kill Riah," he says, his eyes still staring up at the sea.

"Yes."

"I wish I could save her, but you killing her will send her soul to me. You have my word that she will be safe in the afterlife," he says, just as he stands and walks over to me.

"You must enjoy what time you have with your pirates, Cassandra," he says, waving an arm over me, and everything goes black.

I wake up, breathing heavily as I look around at the familiar captain's room on the ship. I take slight comfort in the light snoring of Ryland as he sleeps behind me. I carefully move his arm off my waist, putting it on his side before getting out of the bed. I pull my clothes on and turn back to Ryland. He looks tired, and I don't want to wake him up, but I lean over and kiss his forehead, just over his mark. He doesn't stir, but there is a small lift of his lips, making me smile. I walk out of the room, quietly closing the door behind me and looking up at the sun high in the sky. The deck is full of the people on board, walking around and getting on with the jobs they have. I look around for my other pirates and finally spot Dante sitting with Everly. Dante has a hat on today, likely to protect him from the harsh sunlight. Everly doesn't seem to care, her blonde hair looks almost white as it reflects the light. I walk over, smiling at the pink kitten snuggled up to Everly's chest. It has white ears, but the rest is a light pink colour and is so fluffy that I can't really see its face or eyes. Dante turns towards me, standing up and pulling me to his chest when I'm near.

"Good morning, pretty girl," he says, and I laugh as he kisses my cheek.

"You found the kittens then?" I ask Everly from Dante's arms as he holds me to him, and I wrap my arms around his waist.

"This one found me, actually. She was in my bed, and I checked with Zack about her. He thinks she is a runt of the litter as she is so much smaller than the other kittens."

"Oh no," I say, feeling sorry for the little one.

"I've been feeding her milk and keeping her in my room. Dante and Zack helped me get her a suitable box and food," she says, stroking the tiny kitten's head. I smile at her, knowing she has found a friend for life with her new cat.

"Did you decide a name for her?"

"Nala, it means sweet, which I think suits her," she says and stands up. "I'm going to take her back to my room and keep her warm."

"Is that Thron?" I ask, pointing at the massive island that we are passing by. It is covered in mountains that reach towards the skies and sandy beaches with a few ships pulled up to them.

"Yes. One day, we will come here, and I will show you my favourite beach. The water is so warm, the sand is perfect to build castles, and there are little caves filled with gems we could explore. It's one of my favourites of all the islands," he tells me.

"That sounds perfect, so perfect, pretty boy," I whisper, resting my head against his chest, hearing his calm heartbeat as I watch the island.

Chapter Twenty

Cassandra

"How long until we get to the castle? Or at least near it?" I ask as I stop next to Hunter. His hands are on the wheel as he turns us to the right a little bit. I look around, not seeing anything, other than the sun shining on a few rocks and the sea for miles. How he even knows where we are is a mystery to me, but Hunter seems assured from the controlled look he gives as he looks around. I have hidden my sickness from them all so far, but I know it won't be long until someone sees me throwing up and starts asking questions. I usually sneak out of whoever's bed I'm in and thrown up in the toilet. The only one that has seen me was Hunter, but he hasn't said anything, and it was only the once.

"A day at the most," he states, and points to the sky.

"Someone clearly missed you," he adds, and I follow his direction to see Vivo in the sky, just before she dives down and splashes into the water next to our ship, rocking it a little as water sprays us. I grin, wanting to call her, but she is bigger than the ship, and I don't think she could land on board. I decide to just watch her, knowing she is near is good enough for me.

"We must be getting close to catching up with the army, and she sensed us or something," I say. Hunter nods, watching as Vivo flies back out of the sea and into the air. She circles us for a while, before diving again and this time, coming up with a large fish in her mouth. *Handy trick.*

"I saw you were sick again this morning . . . have you seen Chaz about it? Maybe he could help," Hunter asks me, and I shake my head.

"It's just seasickness," I say, hating the lie that slips out of my mouth so easily. It won't be long until I can tell them all, that's what I keep reminding myself anyway. It's the only way to get through the day.

"You never had sea sickness before," Hunter says and grabs my chin gently, turning my face to look at him. "What are you lying to me about, little bird?"

"Nothing," I say, and he chuckles low, leaning closer and brushing his lips against mine.

"I don't believe you," he whispers.

"You shouldn't, but if you love me, you'll leave it," I plead, and he frowns, letting go of my chin to stroke the back of his hand down my cheek.

"Secrets are not something I like," he says gruffly, his eyes seeming to be fighting with the indecision of asking me or letting it go.

"I wouldn't keep any secret from you unless there was no choice. Please don't ask me to tell you," I almost beg him, staring into his dark-blue eyes and feeling like I'm lost. He nods once, letting go of me to hold onto the wheel.

"Whatever it is, I love you, anyway," he tells me, not looking at me once. I place my hand on his arm for just a second, before walking away and down the small steps to the deck. Dante and Chaz are talking, laughing accusingly as they play cards on a barrel. I see Jacob at the front of the ship, watching where we are going, I expect. My hand goes to my stomach as I watch them all, knowing I could imagine having a baby on this ship. Having a future together, a long and happy one, but I have to do something they may all hate me for. I have to do this alone. It's always been my responsibility. I walk down the steps below deck, finding my way to my room and opening the door, shutting it behind me. I wait until it's gone dark, before grabbing the bag with the crown in, chucking it on my back, and picking up the dagger Jacob gave me.

"Cass? Are you coming for dinner?" Chaz asks, knocking on the door.

"Yes, I will meet you all in there," I say, knowing this is the perfect time to do what I must. They are all distracted. I slide the dagger into the side of my trousers, looking at my ring and my mark on my hand. Guilt fills me for what I have to do, but I don't see any other way of doing this. I quickly decide to write a note, knowing I have to leave something behind, some explanation for them.

For my pirates,
When you know I've left, please don't be mad or angry. I have to face him alone, and I have to do something so evil that I can't have any of you at my side as I do it. Time is running out for us, and I must save what future we have left. Fight for me, for Calais with the army, and I will find you when I have killed him.

187

I love you all. Your Cassandra.

I leave the note on my bed, knowing they might hate me when they read it. But, at least they will be alive. I pull the cloak off the back of the door, putting it on and pulling up my hood. I open my door, sneaking out and looking down the corridor. I can smell Zack's cooking, and I can hear them laughing and talking as they wait for me to come to dinner. I wish I could just go to them, but the crown on my back–the deal made with a god–reminds me that I can't just do that. I turn around, walking up the stairs and pulling the hatch door open. I climb out, closing it behind and looking up at the sky. The sun is setting, but I know Vivo won't be far. I run to the back of the ship, climbing on the very edge of the wood. The ship is moving quick, and the sails are up. I know once I jump, I won't be able to get back on easily.

"Vivo, I need you!" I shout, hoping she hears me, because there is a good chance one of my pirates did. Vivo breaks out of the skies, flying sharply towards me and landing in the sea. I lift my arms above my head and dive into the sea, knowing my dragon will save me.

Chapter Twenty-One

Cassandra

"To the castle, but stay high in the sky. He has a dragon, and we must not be seen," I shout to Vivo as she takes us higher in the skies and away from my ship. I feel my pirates' anger and fear slam into me through my bond. They must have found my note and realised that I'm gone. I look back at my home one more time before we hit the clouds, and place my hand on my stomach. I'm not alone and have everything to fight for. With that renewed determination, I hold on tight to Vivo, and let her fly us straight to the very place I never wanted to return. I have to do this. The king won't expect me to be alone, for me to sneak into the castle and kill the person that gives him his power. The queen. I hold in the tears I feel at the idea of killing her, of

189

taking an innocent soul. *She doesn't deserve this.* I try not to think of anything for the next few hours, just holding onto Vivo. When she dips down, I know we must be close.

"Land near the cliffs, and I will climb up them," I tell her, seeing the light from the castle just under the clouds we are in. She doesn't roar to agree with me, just drops down suddenly, using her wings to glide us around the cliff to the side that is behind the castle. The waves bash harshly against the cliff as she digs her claws into the side, causing me to nearly fall off her. I spot the small ledge to my left, which is clearly where she wants me to climb off.

"Go, my friend, my dragon. You must go now, and thank you," I tell her, hearing her almost purr as I climb off and jump onto the ledge, my arms scraping across the stone. Vivo stares at me, only for a moment, but I know a stare of love when I see one. I never did before meeting my pirates and her, but I do now. She jumps off the cliff, diving into the sea. The moon and the lights from the castle provide the only light in the dark night, as I walk to the edge of the cliff and start climbing up. My foot slips on a rock, and I almost scream as I fall a few steps, but barely manage to hold on. After taking some deep, calming breaths, I remind myself that I can do this. It's just climbing. I keep going, even as the muscles in my arms start to burn, and my body feels exhausted. I finally get to the top, pulling myself up and looking around, thankful to see that it is empty as I crouch down. I look back over the cliff, knowing this is where I fell off. Where the sea god saved me. I doubt he would ever save me again. I stand up, running to the balcony where we escaped last time. I climb on, pressing myself against the wall as I peek into the room. It's empty, and I breathe a sigh of relief. I walk into the room, running over to the door and pressing my ear against it, waiting for any noise.

"I wouldn't do that if I were you," an older female voice says, and a woman steps out of the shadows of the balcony. A guard.

"Pretend you didn't see me?" I request cheekily, standing tall. Her eyes lock on mine, and she stands so very still.

"You are Cassandra, correct?" she asks, and I nod, not seeing any point in lying to her. My mark shows who I am.

"Is my son alive?" she asks.

"Who is your son?" I reply.

"Jacob," she says his name fondly, full of worry, and it suddenly snaps into place as I look at her features.

"You're his mother," I say, and she nods. "He is alive, and married to me. I wouldn't ever ask this, not if I didn't have any other choice. I need to get to the queen, alone." Her eyes widen, and drift to my hand, where she can see my ring and mark.

"Do you love my son?"

"More than I could ever explain. He is one of my chosen," I reply, and just as I speak, I feel the worry, fear, and anger coming from my pirates again.

"You must stay in here for a day," she tells me, and I shake my head, but she carries on speaking. "This room is never used, and there is a cupboard to hide you in. The army is a day away, and when they attack, the queen won't be with the king. It is the only time I can get you to her."

"She will still have guards."

"My husband, and a few of our friends will help you. Why do you need to see the queen?" she asks, and I debate lying to her for a second, but I don't.

"I have to kill her," I answer honestly, and her eyes widen before she looks away.

"There is nothing left but a shell to kill. She is lost and lifeless, anyway. I remember her as the princess, with her princes. Do not feel guilty for putting her out of her misery," she tells me, walking back to the balcony.

"Sleep, you will need the rest, and that door is locked. The only way in is through the balcony, and I will stand watch," she says, leaving me alone. I walk over to the sofa and lie down, pulling out my dagger to hold against my chest. I roll on my side, so I can keep the crown at my back, keeping it safe. I want to reassure my pirates, tell them I'm safe, but my bond doesn't let me. I drift off, with my only thoughts of my pirates to keep the nightmares away.

Chapter Twenty-Two

Ryland

I finish reading Cassandra's note, and throw it back at Chaz who found it, unable to keep looking at the same words over and over.

"She left, and she is going to do this alone. How could she?" I exclaim, slamming my hand on the desk. All the others stare at me; her pirates, Hunter, Jacob, Chaz, Dante, and Zack. None of them have anything to say, and all of us are just as furious.

"Who knew getting her that damn dragon was a bad idea?" Hunter says, rubbing his face with his hand.

"We all did," I say dryly and look down at the map. We should catch up with the army in a day, and be at the castle by tomorrow night, but we won't be able to help her. Not when her dragon will get her there in only a few hours.

"I knew she was keeping secrets, but not what."

"Get Everly in here now, if anyone knows anything, it's her!" I growl out, and Zack is the one that leaves the room. Everyone is silent as we wait for Everly to come here, and tell us what secret Cassandra is hiding from us. I want to be mad at her, angry, but I can't, simply because it would be something I would do in her position. She went to protect us, but it should be all of us that protect her. I look around at my friends, my brother, and see only the triangle mark on her forehead. It reminds me that the sea god will be watching over her. She isn't a normal girl, and I should have guessed her stubbornness would make her do something like this.

"You called?" Everly asks after opening the door and walking in with Zack following.

"What is Cassandra hiding?" I ask her straight away, not wanting to skirt around the bush.

"Why don't you ask *your* wife yourself?" she suggests dryly, holding her hands on her hips.

"Cassandra left and is flying Vivo to the castle," Jacob tells her, and I watch her visibly shocked and worried expression.

"What?" she asks, shaking her head.

"You don't know anything, do you?" I say, walking past her, out of the captain's room and up the steps. I walk straight towards the wheel, leaning against it as I take in the stars, the small islands in the distance, and the silence of the night. There is nothing but the sound of the ship crashing against the water, and the sound of the cold wind pushing the sails.

"I know we have never spoken, and you may not even be listening, but I want to tell you something, Sea God," I say, feeling strange about talking to a god I never believed in. At least I didn't until I saw Cassandra survive falling off a huge cliff and crashing into the sea. "You will protect her, and keep her safe from the danger she is in. I'm not asking you to protect her for me, I'm asking you to protect her because she deserves it. If anyone in this god damn evil world deserves a god's protection, it is her." My words seem to get lost in the sound of the waves, not that I expected an answer. I know she can feel what I do through our bond, but I cannot feel her. I only know she is alive from the bond, but not her emotions.

"She will be safe," I hear a voice whisper, the voice deep, but sounding like it is spoken from the waves. *"But you must be quick."* The voice disap-

pears, but his warning echoes in my mind. I run down the steps, across the deck, and slamming open the cabin door. Everyone stops talking, turning sharply to me.

"We need to throw everything heavy off this ship. We need to be faster," I demand, and Hunter raises an eyebrow at me. "Wake everyone up, that's an order. Our wife needs us, and we must bring the war."

"Aye, captain," Dante says with a grin, getting up and grabbing the box he was sitting on. "Everything?"

"Nothing on this ship is more important than Cassandra, so everything. Someone help me with this table, and someone else get rid of the cannons. We won't need the ship when we get there," I say, and they don't pause as they all get up and start carrying things out of the room. *Hold on for us, our stubborn little pirate.*

Chapter Twenty-Three

Cassandra

I blink my eyes open. My body feels weightless, and I realize I'm floating in warm, still water. My arms are stretched out, and I sit up, seeing the white dress I'm wearing spread out around me in the crystal-blue water. I look around, spotting the sea god sitting on the edge of the pool, his golden hair waving in the breeze. There is nothing else to see, just the cave walls. I swim over, pulling myself out the deep pool and sitting down next to him. The sea god has his eyes closed, his hands folded on his lap as he faces a cave wall.

"It feels like a long time since you have come into my dreams," I muse, and he opens his eyes, not looking at me as he speaks.

"It is the last time. You will die, or live without the help of gods very soon," he explains to me.

"Why did you bring me here?" I ask, ignoring the fact he said I could die. Not very reassuring.

"To say goodbye," he says, and he must feel my shock. "Can gods not have feelings, Cassandra?"

"Do you?" I question him.

"Yes. I love all the children I bless. I love all my own children, but it does not mean I can protect them," he says.

"You have children?" I ask.

"Another story for another day, perhaps?"

"But we will not speak again."

"No, we will not," he comments and looks at me, his eyes glowing a light-blue as he places his hand on my shoulder, but his eyes go to my stomach.

"This is your future, and when you save yourself, you will also save everyone else," he tells me.

"What if I die? What if I can't do this?" I ask, holding a protective hand over my stomach.

"Then everyone dies. The world ends, and only the gods will walk on Calais, but I believe in you," he says, leaning closer and kissing my forehead, right on my mark as everything drifts away into darkness.

. . .

"Wake up, Cassandra!" Someone shakes my shoulder as they whisper the words frantically to me. I blink my eyes open, putting my hand over the dagger and seeing Jacob's mother standing over me. She straightens as I sit up, putting the bag on my lap. I open it up, pulling the crown out, just as I hear the sound of cannons, screams, and dragons roaring, but they are lost in the distance as the power of the crown overwhelms me. I have to shake my head, gaining some kind of control.

"The war has started. It happened earlier than we thought," she says, and I nod. I know my pirates would have rushed in here because of my leaving. I stand up, holding my dagger in one hand and the crown in the other as I follow Jacob's mother to the door. She unlocks it, and we walk out into the large, empty corridor.

"My husband, and those loyal to the princes, have gone ahead to disarm the guards surrounding the queen," she explains to me as we run down the corridor. We run around a corner, and she leads me to a set of stairs. As we run up them, a cannon smashes into the staircase, going straight through the wall.

"Faster, they are destroying the castle," she says, grabbing my arm and pulling me up the stairs around the falling stone. I climb with her, holding on to the dagger and crown even when it's hard to. We come out to another corridor, and it is packed with guards. There are at least ten guards on the floor knocked out. There are five still standing, and they nod at us when they spot us. Jacob's mother runs to one of the guards, holding him close, and I walk past them all, straight towards the closed door.

"The queen is in there, with two maids passed out," one of the guards tells me.

"Thank you." I ask one more thing of them just before I open the door. "Now, do not let anyone in here, please?"

"For the crown and for our children's lives, we will protect the door," the man I presume is Jacob's father says firmly, and the guards move into a line between the door and the only staircase. I take a deep breath before opening the door and going inside. The room is dimly lit with several candles. There are no windows and just a simple bed. On the floor near the door are two brown-haired girls, their heads hung down, so I can't see their faces. I can hear that they're breathing, so I know they are okay. The queen sits on the bed, her long, almost-black hair hiding her face.

"Queen Riah?" I ask, but she doesn't move. She

doesn't even flinch at my calling her name. I look down at the dagger, swallowing the nervousness that builds up in my throat as I walk over to her. I go around her, sitting next to her on the bed, when she suddenly stands up. I stand up, too, facing her as she raises her blue eyes to meet mine. She looks so pale, so thin and lost. Her eyes, though, they are the image of Hunter's.

"You have his eyes," I say, not realising I've even spoken out loud until she nods.

"I-I can't do it," I say, dropping the crown and the dagger onto the floor, staying still as they bounce on the wood before settling. The sounds of dragons roaring, swords smashing against each other, and screams can be heard outside. Yet, the room is eerily silent in a way. Queen Riah keeps her eyes locked with mine, not blinking, not moving. She is like a doll, no fear ever shows in her eyes as I face her with a dagger. Not even when it is clear I came here to kill her. Her lips mumble something, nothing that I can make out as actual words. I watch her lean down, and pick the crown up, a glow floating up her arms, and her mark lights up a glowing blue colour.

"You must let me die. You have to save the future, you have to save the sea, Cassandra," she insists, and it's the most I've ever heard her speak.

Maybe the crown is giving her some power, power she is using to speak to me normally. To get past the damage that has been done to her by a man she once loved and trusted.

"You're their mother, and I *love* them. I can't do that to them," I say, taking a deep breath. When I need to be strong, when I need to be emotionless, I'm not. I can't do this, and it will cost me everything.

"You love my sons, they are your chosen," she says, and looks down at the crown for a long while. I don't answer her, she knows the answer, anyway.

"They are fighting the king now, with my other chosen and my army. They don't know I'm here, what I came to do," I explain to her, hating that I had to make this decision without them. *And I still couldn't do it.*

"They wouldn't stop you. It's time I died, and you will send my evil chosen after me. I will make sure he pays in death, his soul will burn with the god of souls in hell," she exclaims. I believe her completely, seeing the determination in her eyes. She looks up, her eyes so much like Ryland's as she smiles, and her mouth parts in shock. She coughs, and blood trickles out her mouth as I look down, and see the end of a long dagger appearing through her stomach.

"Finally, I get to be with my chosen," she chuckles as the dagger is pulled out. "Not that they ever left me," she whispers as her eyes fade, and her soul leaves her body. She falls suddenly, and I catch her, holding her to me as I look up and see who killed the queen.

"You . . . . How could it be you?" I mutter, shaking my head as Livvy drops the dagger on the floor and takes a step back.

"He never killed me, and I owed you. We are even now, Cassandra. Please don't stop me from leaving," she says, walking towards the door. I gently place the queen on the floor, closing her eyes and picking the crown up.

"Stop! I deserve more of an explanation from you," I shout at Livvy as she rests her hand on the door handle.

"I am done. I should have died at the hands of whoever won me at the auctions, but I did not. I believe you only saved my life because I was meant to help you now. To do something no one else could," she opens the door slightly. "The king will be weak now, and he won't have his gifts. You can finally win." Her last words end on a scream, as the door falls away from a massive blast that sends me flying across the room, landing next to the bed which slides away. I panic, reaching around as I fall and grab hold of a floor board, waiting for the rocking to stop. When the dust settles, half the room is gone, and the walls don't exist anymore. I look across the battlefield, seeing thousands of guards and my people fighting. There are hundreds of ships, some are sinking, while others are on fire in the sea. I look up, seeing the king riding his dragon, flying across the sky and burning the ships. Even without his gifts, he is still burning everything.

"Vivo!" I scream out, placing the crown on my head.

Chapter Twenty-Four

Hunter

I almost drop my swords when everyone stops to watch the castle fall to pieces. The sound of my father's dragon snaps me out of it, knowing I can't die. I can feel Cassandra is alive, and that's all that matters. I look around and see fire, death, and destruction everywhere. There is so much of it. I spot Everly fighting back to back with Chaz against four other guards, and they need help. I lift my sword, chucking it straight towards the guard nearest me, and it goes straight through him. I run over, pulling it out of his back before he can even fall to the floor. Everly continues to struggle against two guards, and one of them manages to knock her to the ground. Tyrion comes running, colliding with him, and pushing him away. I run over, but I'm too late to stop the guard from stabbing his sword into Everly's leg, making her scream. I kick him off of her, stabbing him in his chest before he can get up. Chaz finishes off the other guard with her sword, and I see Tyrion is dealing with the last guard just fine.

"Chaz, she needs you!" I shout to him, kneeling down as she screams and holds her leg. Chaz runs over, taking my place as I stand to keep an eye out for anyone coming near.

"We need to wrap this, and it's going to hurt," Chaz warns Everly, pulling out the bottom of his shirt and ripping a long bandage from it.

"Do it!" she demands, closing her eyes, and I spot a guard running towards us. I smack my sword against the guard's as I hear Everly's scream behind me. He watches me from under his helmet, and it suddenly seems to dawn on him who I am as he fights harder. I smack my elbow into his face, knocking him to the ground and slamming my sword into his chest.

"Vivo!"

"Did you hear that?" I ask, looking up to see a tiny part of the castle left standing and Cassandra standing on it, glowing a blue colour, and the crown is on her head.

"She is going to fight the king with her dragon!" I

growl out, knowing how dangerous her reckless decision is, but I have to believe in her. I look around, seeing the changed ones using their gifts to throw guards into the sea, but most of the guards are running to the decks and trying to kill everyone there instead. I run back to Everly, who Tyrion has managed to pick up, and Chaz stands near them. I look around, seeing Ryland near the cliff, and Jacob and Zack protecting some of the changed ones.

"Can you walk?" I ask Everly, and she shakily lifts her sword.

"I can."

"No, you can't. You need to rest or you might do serious damage to your leg," Chaz warns, placing his hand on her shoulder, but she shakes him off.

"I can fight."

"Then you will, and I will be at your side," Tyrion promises her, and she nods, barely able to remain standing. I share a look with Chaz, and we both agree without words that we need to keep Everly alive. Not just because she is to be queen at the end of this, but because Cassandra will kill us if we let anything happen to her.

"Let's do this," I shout, lifting my sword, and running head-first into the biggest crowd of guards I can find.

Chapter Twenty-Five

Cassandra

I jump on Vivo's back when she gets to me, and hold on tight so I don't fall off as she takes off towards the battlefield. I can sense my pirates, and I send them the only feeling I know they might need. Love. I spot other changed ones using their powers in the fight below. Someone is using fire, another is making large plants rip out of the ground, and vines are grabbing guards. I look back at the castle, just as more cannons are fired into it. The ships are behind the cliffs, firing cannon after cannon at the castle, or what is left of it now.

"We need to fight the king and his dragon. Fire must be destroyed!" I shout to Vivo, who roars, gaining the attention of the king and his dragon as we get closer. They turn around, and the king's eyes lock with mine, a sinister grin spreading over his lips as his eyes burn with anger. I try not to be frightened, but some fear still fills me as I remember what he did to me. I close my eyes for just a second, and remind myself that this is his ending, not mine. He lifts his hand as I open my eyes, and his dragon breathes a long stream of fire straight at us. Vivo roars, and a long breeze of icy wind comes from her mouth, hitting the fire right in the middle of us both. Vivo pushes the dragon's fire away, her strength is too much for it to keep up with. The fire dragon stops suddenly, flying straight towards us and knocking its huge body into Vivo. I scream as I try to hold on. Both of the dragons claw at each other, and I can't lift my head from the pressure of the wind to look at the king or anything that is going on. A loud roar fills my ear, and then the dragons hit the ground, sending me flying off the dragon and rolling across the grass. I groan in agony, feeling my shoulder hurting me, and my right leg is shooting with pain. I bite my lip as I grab the crown near my head, shakily standing up and looking around. I can see all my pirates fighting in the distance, and the dragons are back in the sky, battling with each other. I don't know who is winning, but they are covered in blood. I spot the king near the edge of the cliff, and no one is here to stop me from getting to him. I run over, avoiding the few bodies on the floor until I'm close enough to him.

I stand on the edge of the cliff, holding the blood-covered crown. The crown we fought so long to get. The crown that will win this war. I glance around at the men I love, each one of them I would die to protect. My pirates are fighting all around me on the battlefield, keeping me alive as I face the king alone. This was always the plan, the only one that would work. The ground shakes as more screams fill the night. I can't look away from the king to see if anyone I know is dying. If anyone I love is.

Everything we have fought for has led us to this moment, and I won't let them down.

We don't say any words to each other, as words are not needed. He knew this was coming, and the war around us is proof. The king started this, not me. I was chosen to stop this.

"You will never save the seas," the king sneers at me after a long silence between us.

"I don't need to. The Sea God will save us all," I say, my voice loud as the wind howls, and lightning fills the skies.

"What did you promise him in return?" he shouts back at me. I look the king over, remembering every cruel thing he has done to me, the people he has taken from me, and the deaths he has caused.

"Your death," I say and lift the crown, placing it on my head, and the power floods my mind.

"Kill me, and you will have my soul tarnishing yours forever," he says, opening his arms.

"This is for my mother," I hear said next to me, and I turn facing Ryland as he steps to my side, throwing his dagger, and it lands perfectly in the centre of the king's chest.

"No!" the king blurts out, staring at the dagger and lifting his hands in shock.

"You have no power now," I say, and close my eyes, remembering his shock. I lift my hands slowly, pulling as much water as I can from the sea. When I open them, a wall of water is hanging over the cliff, the king standing right next to it. The crown lets me control the sea, control everything. I can feel the power, so much power.

"Cassandra, stay with us. Remember why you have the crown, and why you are here," Ryland coaxes from somewhere near me, and I open my eyes, looking at him.

"I remember," I say, lifting my blue glowing hand. I look down to see all of my body is glowing blue before looking back at the king.

"Return to the sea, and meet your fate," are the last words I give him before he screams as I let the sea pull him back over the cliff. There is a deadly silence as I still hold the wall of water and turn around. I see Vivo sitting on what is left of the castle, all frozen over from her power, and the king's dragon frozen at her feet, clearly dead. *We have won.* All my pirates walk over to me, many of them covered in blood and cuts, but alive. That's all that matters. I spot Everly as she comes over, with Tyrion holding her up as her leg bleeds. I use my water to lift myself into the air, until I'm standing above every person on this field.

"The king is dead!" I shout, and cheers follow my words. I wait for them to stop before carrying on. "This land will be known as the final fight between our people. The final war. We will have peace!" I shout, and the people cheer again. I watch as the guards, the changed ones, and the rebellion army all fall to their knees. I pull some more water over, lifting Everly into the air as she lets go of Tyrion. She stands tall, despite the blood pouring down her leg.

"Rise, Queen Everleigh. Queen of Calais!" I shout, going to my knee in the water and lowering my head. Everyone shouts her name, cheering about their new queen, but I keep my eyes below me, on my pirates as they smile.

Hunter mouths one word. "Home."

I lower myself and Everly back down to the ground, before pulling the crown off but keeping hold of the water.

"I need to do this, return the gift that was stolen from the sea. I must finish the deal," I tell Chaz who gets to my side first.

"We do this together. We are here," Jacob says, and the others all stay close, their actions making it clear they are in this with me. I walk to the very edge of the cliff, holding the crown over it, and place it in the risen water.

"I never thanked you for your gift, and I don't mean the powers. I mean the bond. Thank you for my soul mates, and thank you for blessing me. The sea god will never be feared again, only worshipped. That is my promise to you. Goodbye," I say, and I let the crown fall with the sea as the power leaves me. I watch as the water drops back down, and the tornadoes, whirlpools, and the anger of the Storm Sea disappears, only leaving peace. The next thing I feel is myself falling back as darkness takes over.

Chapter Twenty-Six

Cassandra

"Queen Everleigh of Calais, you are crowned, and you will serve Calais. Do you accept your birthright?" Master Light asks Everly as she kneels in front of him, the three other masters, and me. Her long red dress circles around her like she is kneeling in a cloud of sparkling fabric. The red represents the new royal symbol, a red rose. The old royal colour of green has been erased, and red is the new colour. Everly chose red to represent the amount of blood that was lost to secure the throne.

"I accept my birthright," she replies, and he lowers the red ruby crown onto her head. The thousands of people gathered around cheer for their new queen as she stands, the official crowning finally over. The castle was destroyed, nothing but rubble and blood was left. We managed to pull many surviving guards out of the castle, like Jacob's parents, but Livvy's body was found near the queen's. She must have died when the castle fell. Hunter and Ryland know how their mother died, and they don't blame me for wanting to go alone. They were glad that it wasn't me that killed her in the end though. We had a funeral for them all, a funeral that thousands of people attended. My baby kicks, and I smooth my hands over my rather large bump as Everly smiles at me and turns around, raising her hands in the air to stop the cheering.

"Thank you for your support," she says first. "I am not like any queen, or any royal, that we have had before us. I was brought up on Onaya, starved for most my life, and my story's past was nothing good. We as a world have suffered, Calais has suffered, and I will spend the rest of my life making sure that we suffer no more! Calais will be strong, changed ones will be safe, and *everyone* will know true peace," she stops her speech as cheers roll out, and she walks down the gap in the people, limping on her right leg that never fully recovered from the war. The healers and changed ones have tried to heal her, with no luck. Everly doesn't talk about the limp now, but I know she is in pain when she walks. I nod respectfully at her four new personal guards, who follow her until she disappears out of sight.

"A grand party, full of dancing and celebration is to be had! Enjoy!" Master Pirate says, pulling a blonde woman to his side who grins up at him. We lost a lot of people in the war, thousands from both the king's army and our own. The changed ones saved a lot of people using their powers, and everyone is looking at them in a different light. The first thing Everly did was to make a law stating that changed ones are free, and any changed one that needs a home has one in her mountains.

"Thank you for everything, but I believe I heard you will be leaving us soon," Master Light says quietly from my side. I didn't notice him move next to me, as I was lost in my own thoughts and happiness. My pirates reacted worse than I thought when I told them about the baby. They all got mad about me fighting the king and riding a dragon while pregnant. But once Chaz looked me over and told them that me and the baby were fine, they soon all became as delighted as I am. And then, they became the overprotective pirates that they are today.

"This is not my home, not my baby's, nor my husbands'," I say gently, not meaning any offense, but

I know where my home is. This is the last day in the mountains for me.

"Then safe travels, Cassandra. Know you are always welcome in the mountains as a master. The people will never forget the changed one from Onaya that changed *everything*," Master Light says, placing his hand on my shoulder for a second before he walks away into the crowd. I walk through the middle, stopping a few times to speak to some people before moving to leave the room. My pirates are waiting at the door, standing in a line almost, and each one of them looks relaxed, happy.

"Time for us to leave. Have you told her yet?" Hunter asks as I get to him first, and he wraps his arms around me.

"She already knows," Everly's voice comes from behind me before I can answer Hunter's question. I turn to see her standing watching me, with open arms.

"Say goodbye, little bird," Hunter whispers behind me, and I run to Everly, hugging her tight, even though my large bump gets in the way.

"Go and enjoy your life with your pirates. Just please come back sometime. I want to meet this little one, and I will miss you," Everly says, placing her hand on my bump. It's harder than I thought it would be to leave her here, but I know this is her story and not mine. Everly is one of the strongest people I know, and she doesn't need me. My story was always to get her here, and to set my people free. Now it's time for me to enjoy what I fought for.

"Nothing could keep me away," I promise her, and she nods, wiping her tears away.

"Be safe," she whispers, and I hug her once more, whispering, so only she can hear.

"I am so proud of you, my lovely sister, and the true queen you were always meant to be." I pull away before she can reply and walk over to my pirates, knowing we are finally free.

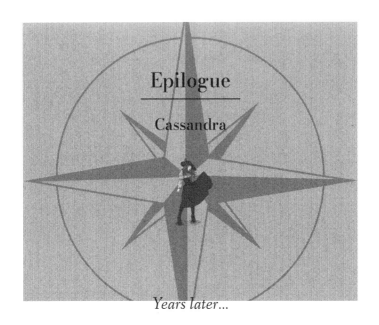

Epilogue

Cassandra

Years later...

"Riah! Get down from there, you could fall!" I shout at my daughter, as she swings like a monkey on the ropes hanging off the sail. She is always climbing something, that girl.

"I will get her," I hear Jacob say behind me with an amused tone. I smile as he pulls himself up, grabbing our daughter who laughs and jumps on his back. He climbs back down, putting the naughty little five-year-old on the deck. She grins up at me, her dark-blue eyes proclaiming innocence like I didn't just find her climbing again. She looks so much like me in some ways, with her brown hair in braids, and her changed one mark on her forehead. Riah's is a crown, and I was shocked when she was born with it.

"Dinner is ready, and you know your dads will be mad if you are late to dinner again," I tell her, and she huffs, rolling her little eyes at me. I try not to laugh as she picks up her little pirate hat, putting it on, and stomping off.

"Stubborn, brave, and fearless. Who does our daughter remind me of?" Jacob asks, and I laugh, shrugging.

"No idea," I say, wrapping my arms around him. I watch the water sway in the distance, the calm peacefulness of the sea, and the sight of Vivo flying around Onaya which we have just left.

"This is everything I could have ever dreamed of," I say quietly, and Jacob kisses my forehead as my bond flares to life with happiness and joy.

"Everything was worth the fight, for the life we now have."

About the Author

G. Bailey is a USA Today bestselling author of books that are filled with everything from dragons to pirates. Plus, fantasy worlds and breath-taking adventures. Oh, and some swoon-worthy men that no girl could forget. G. Bailey is from the very rainy U.K. where she lives with her husband, two children and three cheeky dogs. And, of course, the characters in her head that never really leave her, even as she writes them down for the world to read!

Please feel free say hello on here or head over to Facebook to join G. Bailey's group, Bailey's Pack! (Where you can find exclusive teasers, random giveaways and sneak peeks of new books!)

Join Bailey's Pack on Facebook to stay in touch with
the author, find out what is coming out next,
exclusive giveaways and spoilers!

Bonus Read

Want a free shifter book to read? Click here.

There is no place for love in a world of vampires who own your soul.

On Riona Dark's twenty-second birthday, being kidnapped by strangers in the night was *not* the surprise party she was expecting.

Riona is taken to the hidden world of vampires, a remote island called The Onyx, where being human means you are less than nothing. Locked up with other humans, Riona finds out that she will soon be sold at The Auction.

When two vampire princes, with dark eyes and even darker souls, come to view her and the others, Riona knows the vampires here are just as dangerous as they are gorgeous.

Once sold, Riona is told that her life belongs to the vampires who own her. They will own her soul, mind and body. *Resisting means only death.*

Riona won't be sold without a fight, and the only power in The Onyx is blood, desire...and death.

Warning: This book is a dark romance, and it contains themes not for the faint of heart.

Chapter 27

Bonus Read

M y dream turned into a nightmare the moment I saw his dark eyes.

The suncatcher above me spins in the light breeze, catching beams of light and reflecting them in a million different strands of colour all across my dorm room and waking me up far too early than should be allowed. That pretty but annoying thing was a gift from my brother, and he rarely gets me anything nice, so I had to keep it.

"It's your goddamn twenty-second birthday, and you're still in bed!" my roommate, aka Miss Noisy and Perky First Thing in the morning, shouts across our room as I squeeze my eyes shut. I groan and pull my covers over my head, hoping that she will bugger off, but there is no such luck as I hear her footsteps coming closer. Snatching my sheet from me, she flicks on my bedside lamp to make it that much brighter in here. I peel my eyes open and glare at her as she leans over me, hands on her hips.

"Can your birthday present to me be a lie-in? Please, Sophie?" I grumble with the best impression of puppy dog eyes I can give. Sophie Devert is one year older than I am, about four levels crazier, and overall my best friend in the world since middle school. Pushing her bright autumn red hair behind her ear, she steps back and stretches, showing off her slim and toned body. That's what you get for being a pro swimmer. My short ass body reflects my art major *all* too well. I slide out of bed and make my way to the bathroom, shutting the door behind me. After a quick shower, I towel dry my waist-length, mousy blonde hair and then wrap myself in the towel before heading back out. On my made-up bed is a present box with a big pink bow. It must be my birthday if Sophie is cleaning anything at all.

I chuckle as I sit down and open up the box, pulling out a short, light pink dress and matching light pink heels in my size. I might not be the girliest girl out there, but I love pink as much as I love dressing up for one night. Sophie is practically jumping on the spot in excitement, waiting for my response. She knows she did well; the girl knows me better than I know myself.

"I love them! Thank you so much, Soph!"

"I knew you would!" She gives me a brief hug. "Now we just have to wait for that brother of yours to call and tell you the next gift," she replies as she picks up her bag with a cheeky grin. "See you at lunch?"

"Same place as usual?" I question as I place the dress back in the box and the heels too.

"As always," she confirms with a wink before leaving the room. After she is gone, I get myself dressed in skinny jeans and a white top with criss-cross patterns cut into the shoulders. As I pull my boots on, my phone rings with the damn cat screeching noise my brother put on it as a joke and I haven't been able to change. I jump, like I do every single damn time, and answer it without looking, popping it onto loudspeaker.

"Happy birthday!" my mum and dad shout down the phone at the same time. Just hearing them makes me smile, the cat ringtone forgotten. "Can we FaceTime?"

"Sure!" I answer, finishing with my boots and switching the call to FaceTime. When the camera comes on, I can only see my reflection for a second, my big doe-like blue eyes and round face that Sophie always says makes me look like a Barbie doll. I've always taken offence to that...but she is right. Eventually, the camera catches up, and I get a close up of the side of my mum's nose. "Mum, you need to hold it away. I can't see you, remember?"

"Oh right," she grumps, not liking to be called out for her terrible tech skills. She pulls the camera back, and even though they are very close, it's good enough. My mother's grey hair is perfectly styled in curls around her wrinkled face, and she has a cream cardigan on with her pearl necklace she never takes off. My dad is in one of his classic sweater vests, and his greying brown hair is swept to the side. He smiles at me and pushes his glasses back up his nose.

"Where is your brother? Has he not come over with his gift yet?" Mum asks, well, demands to know.

Being the overprotective sister I am, I lie. "Of course he has. Austin just had to get to class."

Total lie.

"Well, I'm glad he is looking after you there. I do worry about you," Mum says with her usual overly worried tone. "Did our gift get to yours yet? It's not much, but we never know what to get you."

"No, but I will check my post in a bit," I reply, drifting my gaze to my dad. "How are you, dad?"

"Happy to see my little girl," he replies with soft eyes. Mum is the tough one, and my dad is as laid back as it comes. Together, they really do make the best parents. "I struggle to understand how you are twenty-two. It feels like yesterday that you were just a baby who slept in my arms, sucking her thumb."

My cheeks light up.

"We will let you go and try calling Austin again. Honestly, that boy never answers his phone," she huffs. Yeah, that's because he is a dick and likely hungover once again. I don't say that though, not wanting my parents to know the truth, and I just smile before saying my goodbyes. Deciding to find my twin brother and give him his gift is the best idea this morning, as I'm totally skipping class since it's my birthday, so I head out of my room after grabbing my hoodie and bag. I pull my hoodie on and swing my bag over my shoulder, running down the stairs to the post boxes. Finding my key in my bag, buried deep under all the very important shit I keep in there, I open up the letterbox and find three letters. I open them on my way to my brother's dorm room, not surprised to see a birthday card from my parents with three hundred pounds inside. Awesome. I push that letter into my bag and open the second one, which is another birthday card with a red rose on the front. Inside, I quickly read the long paragraph.

"My sweet niece, Riona,
Ri-Ri, it's been a long time since I've written to you,
but as always, I ask for you to follow my advice. Do
not leave your dorm tonight, it is not safe at Aberdeen
University on this particular night. They are out
hunting, and they will not be able to resist your blood.
Trust me for once, and have a good birthday.
I will come when it is safe to do so. It is time we
spoke.

As always,
Your uncle

Another card from my father's particularly insane brother, who I've not seen since I was eight. I only remember overhearing a conversation my parents had with him, something about blood and sacrifices. Either way, I overheard enough to know he had lost his goddamn mind. I push the letter back in and find the third one isn't addressed to me at all, it's for Austin. Finally I get to the guys' dorm and head around the back, knowing I can't just walk in, thanks to their stupid rules. No girls allowed...even if there are, no doubt, quite a few girls in this place with their boyfriends. Two trees climb the side of the building, and I climb the left one, pushing myself onto a branch. Bracing myself, I jump to the next tree and keep climbing up until I'm near the top of the tree and the single branch that is close to the ledges of the windows. Ignoring the fear of falling, because damn that would hurt, I carefully crawl across the large branch and onto the ledge of the window. The cold winter wind whips around my body, and I'm thankful there is no ice on the ledge as I push the window up and climb inside, knocking off a pile of books.

"Nice to see you as always, Ria."

I pause and turn my gaze to the half-naked guy in his bed, sheets pooled around his waist, the flickering sunlight from behind me kissing the skin of his chest. Arlo O'Dargan. Aka my brother's best friend and my long-time frenemy since first school. His deep voice is annoyingly perfect, much like the rest of him. Sun-kissed blond hair, bright topaz-green eyes, and a jawline any model would be jealous of, he could be classed as the perfect guy. Just not to me. I don't see him like that, not even as I glance at his rock-hard abs and big shoulders. Nope.

Dammit, I got the wrong room again.

I glare at him. "I wish I could say the same, Arlo. I'm surprised you're even in your own bed and not in some poor girl's."

"None of the girls' beds I join are poor or unhappy, Ria-banana-llama," he teases and stands up, not giving one shit that he only has boxers on. I sharply turn away and blindly stumble to his door, grabbing the handle.

"And don't call me that!" I shout back.

"Make me stop then!" he hollers to my back as I slip out of his door and slam it hard behind me, hearing his laugh in the corridor. Taking a few steps, I find the right door and bang on it a few times before opening it up. I flick the light on as I walk in and see my brother snoring in bed. The shower is on, so he isn't alone (unlucky girl), and I walk right up to him, stepping over messy clothes and empty beer bottles.

"Asshole, wake up!" I shout, kicking his leg that's hanging out of the bed. He jolts up, brushing a hand through his dark blond hair and relaxing when he sees it is me. For twins, we are pretty different. For one, my brother is well over six foot, and he has brown eyes. He looks like he got all the good genes and I was cut short at some point with my height. And generally, I'm not as popular as he is, mostly because Austin could charm his way out of a lion's den even if he was a gazelle. I'd definitely be eaten by the lion in under three seconds flat.

"Happy birthday, twin sis!" he holds his hand up for a high five.

"Happy birthday right back to you. Did you forget our plans for breakfast today?" I ask, and his sheepish grin says it all as I high-five him. "Oh, and answer your phone. Mum and dad have been calling and then nagging me because you didn't answer."

"Of course," he replies with a wave of his hand like it isn't an issue. "Wanna get breakfast now?"

I glance at the bathroom door and back to Austin, arching an eyebrow. "What about your guest?"

"I don't even know her name, to be honest with you, sis," he answers, and I pull a face at him as he shoves his shoes on. He writes a quick note for shower girl before hooking his arm around my shoulder and guiding me out of his stinky room. After a short walk to the cafeteria, we both sit down with our coffees and relax.

"The party is at eight. I did remember it's my year to host," he states, crossing his arms. One good thing about being a twin? Sharing the responsibility of hosting the party. Last year, I spent months planning a massive rave in an abandoned castle. I damn well hope Austin has come up with something good, or I'm having our next party next year in a farm with pigs. "It's going to be the most epic party."

I grin. "Where is it then?"

"On the beach, the left side, you know where there is that cavern?" he questions, and I nod, feeling excited. "Well, be there at eight, sis, and I'll give you a gift then."

"I will be there," I reply, knowing the lazy ass hasn't been shopping yet and plans to the second he leaves the cafe. I reach into my bag and hand him the small box and the letter that came to me. He pops open the box and pulls out the silver and black bead bracelet I made for him in class. The beads are all made from quartz, our birthstone, and the middle one has his initials carved into it.

"This is seriously fucking awesome," he tells me, sliding it on his wrist and doing it up. "Did you make it?"

"Yup. Now go and buy me something pink and expensive," I say, climbing to my feet. "Oh, and make sure there is wine at the party. White wine, I don't like red."

"You got it," he replies, and I chuckle as I leave and head for class. Tonight is going to be epic, that's for sure.

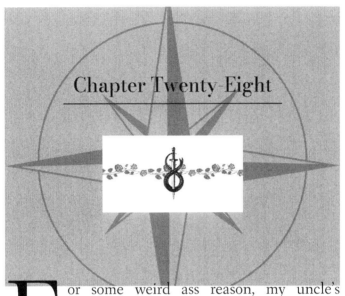

Chapter Twenty-Eight

For some weird ass reason, my uncle's warning comes into my mind as I look at myself in the mirror. My pink dress fits my body like a glove, emphasizing all my curves, and my heels make me seem taller than I am at just five foot five. I've taken a ridiculous amount of time curling all my hair, only to brush the curls out to make it seem like my hair is naturally wavy. *Girl Problems 101*. As soon as someone invents a quicker way to get this effect, the better. Still, my uncle's warning makes me halt and actually almost want to stay in. I mean, he is old and literally insane, but his warning has still creeped me the hell out. I wonder if Austin got one of those cards. I really should have asked him today.

"Are you finally going to live out all the brother's

best friend romance novels I've read, and hook up with Arlo?" Soph asks with a small grin, coming out of the bathroom, looking ready to kill in a short leather skirt and a yellow crop top that hides pretty much none of her. Her bright hair is up in a ponytail, and her makeup, although light, is bang on. I can never get my makeup that perfect.

I screw up my face. "You're gross. Arlo is—"

"Ridiculously hot *and* single," Soph interrupts. He might be all those, but that wasn't what I was going to say. "And he only has eyes for you."

"You're just talking out of your arse now," I mutter, picking up my phone. "Come and take a selfie with me before we leave."

She chuckles and rushes to my side, and we take several photos before posting them on Instagram. While I'm on there, I find several photos of my brother at the party and the dozens of bottles of white wine he has left on the beach for me. That alone makes me grin as we grab our bags and head out. The dorm is pretty empty of other students as we head down the stairs and out the front doors. The air is cold now, and I instantly wish I had brought a coat, but then again, I will be in front of a bonfire soon, by the looks of the photos. Soph hooks her arm in mine and rests her head on my shoulder as we head down the pathway towards her car. She has rich as hell parents, and their idea of a gift was the shiny new red Land Rover, and I'm the lucky bitch who is her bestie, so I can take full advantage of the heated seats. Soph opens her bag and searches for her keys, and then keeps searching, looking more frustrated by the second.

"Crap, I forgot my phone," she mutters and pauses, closing her bag with her keys in her hand, the glittery elephant keyring I bought her shining from the street light. "Why don't you drive my car there, and I will grab an Uber."

"I can wait for you," I say, even as I glance at my own phone and see that we are ten minutes late to my own party.

"Nope. Just go," she says, passing me the keys. "I want to call my mum anyways, check and see how she is doing today."

She looks down, and I place my hand on her arm, wishing I could help. Her dad buys her cars, and her mum is one pill away from forgetting who she is half the time. Money doesn't bring happiness, that's for sure. Soph's life makes me happy for my middle-class upbringing, everything from the pound ice lollies I loved from the shops to the budget beach holidays in a tiny caravan in Wales.

"Okay, see you in a bit," I reply, leaning forward and kissing her cheek.

"Don't jump Arlo until I get there! I wanna be there when I'm proven right!" she shouts over her shoulder as she walks away. Bitch. My cheeks are still red as I glance around, seeing no one in the parking lot. I laugh as I climb into Soph's car, pushing a bag of gym clothes into the passenger seat and closing the door behind me. After doing my seat belt up and, most importantly, putting the heated seats on, I head straight towards the beach. I'm thankful there is no traffic around at this time of day. By the time I park in the beach car park, I'm half an hour late, and I know Austin is going to be mad.

Thank god it is our birthday.

Climbing out of my car with my bag, I lock up as I hear the distant music of the party and smell a bonfire mixed in with the smell of the sea. Austin knows me well, this is the perfect party for me, considering the beach is my favourite place in the world. There is something so calming about looking at the sea, watching the waves wash in and out across the sand. Even when there is a storm, there is always the peace right after. The sea is my happy place, it always has been since I was a kid. It's the only place I feel myself and safe. That's why when I'm older, I'm buying a house as close to the sea as I possibly can get.

The rickety wooden steps eventually give out to just sand, and I slip off my heels, sinking my toes into the soft damp sand.

"Goldilocks, goldilocks, are you lost?"

I spin around to find the man who spoke, but there is no one here, just the sounds of the party and the waves of the sea.

"Dance for me, goldilocks. Spin and spin and spin until your head comes right off."

I turn around again and search everywhere, not hearing or seeing anyone as my heart starts pounding in my chest.

Run, Ria.

Hearing my brother's voice in my head like he is right next to me, I take off down the beach path, rushing towards the party where I know I will be safe. I drop my heels and bag so I can run faster, and just as I see the party, the crowd of shadows around the bonfire in the far distance, I breathe out a sigh of relief.

Then hands wrap around my waist and a hand grabs my throat, arching my neck to the side with a jolt that takes my breath away. Something sharp suddenly bites into my neck, digging in deep, and I scream when I realise it's teeth. I don't stop scream-ing, the pain indescribable, even as I go into shock and almost numb to what is happening to me. The world becomes fuzzy, and my screams fade into cries as my legs go out from under me. The man biting me, holding me, holds me up by my waist, and the world begins to spin.

"Don't kill her!" I hear another man shout. "That's enough!"

The man holding me seems to grumble into my neck, seconds before his teeth leave my neck, and he spins me around, grabbing my chin. Even as I black out, I hear his words and see my blood dripping down his chin as the last thing I can focus on.

"Yes, my masters will love you. You taste like heaven."

Chapter Twenty-Nine

"Wake up before you fall over!" a girl's voice drags into my mind, and I groggily blink my eyes open, feeling a sharp pain in my neck as I breathe in the smell of saltwater, sweat and the metallic tang of blood. It's freezing cold and damp all around me, and with only my small pink dress on and no shoes, my toes feel close to falling off. My lips are dry, but my wet, cold clothes cause me to start shaking almost immediately. My hand shoots to my neck where the pain is, only for me to realise I have iron cuffs wrapped around my wrists, with a chain going through the holes, connecting me to the floor and stopping me from lifting my hands above my waist. Fear renders me silent as I search around the room, seeing other faces in the darkness but not being able to make out much about them. The same girl who woke me up speaks again. "Don't scream, no one comes, and if they do, it's those men who took us, and they aren't nice. They just bite."

Every vivid memory of the beach comes back to haunt me. The screams, the pain in my neck, and the overwhelming sense of fear that crawled into my system like a drug.

"Where are we? What the hell is that thing that attacked me?" I question, wriggling on the wooden crate I'm sitting up on, my back plastered to the side of a curved wooden wall. The room seems to slightly rock, I notice, in the silence that follows as the girl doesn't answer me back. I don't hear anything outside this room, but the smell of saltwater and the rocking movement suggests we are on a ship or boat. I wonder how long. "Please answer."

"I was at a party on a beach, invited by some other friends even though I don't go to many parties...," she starts, her voice ringing with fear. That was my party, the one I never got to. Oh my god. My parents must be going mad with worry, and Austin? Was Austin taken? "The men...no, *monsters*, attacked the party and killed so many of my friends as I tried to run. One caught me and bit my neck, and

I passed out. I woke up here the same as you but a few hours earlier. There was another girl in with us, but she wouldn't stop screaming, and one of the monsters came in here... He bit her neck and dragged her out."

They killed everyone at the party bar a few. What if they only kept women?

They might have killed Austin. The thought lingers in my mind like an unwanted visitor, repeating itself again and again until I can't breathe with pure panic. If the girl with me notices my panic, she doesn't say anything, just leans back and looks up at the small bits of light shining through the planks of wood on the ceiling. Austin. My twin brother. He might be gone. And Sophie? What if she got to the party when it was still being attacked? Did they take her? Or kill her too? No. I can't think like that. If they took me, they might have taken them, and then there is a chance we will all survive wherever we are going to.

I'm going to make sure of it. Clearly, these monsters who took me live on blood, and mine seems to have delighted the guy who bit me. I bet they won't expect their food to bite back. Wherever they take us, there must be a way out, and then I only need to find a normal person and scream for help.

I straighten in my seat, yawning a little, and my breaths come out like puffs of smoke. "They must be vampires. You know from movies and books? I mean, who else would drink blood?"

"The blood-sucking did kinda give that hint," the girl replies with a small laugh that soon dies away into pity for our situations. "I didn't even read paranormal books, I much prefer contemporary. Now this?"

We both stare at each other, the fear and horror of the situation hitting home. I did read paranormal and fantasy books because I prefer the escape from reality that contemporary doesn't usually give me. But I didn't expect to be right smack in the middle of one of the many books I read. I wonder what these vamps are like. Are they the bad guys in the books? The monsters?

Does that make me a captive? My heart starts pounding as I begin to panic, and I suck in air, trying to think of anything else other than where I am.

"Tell me something before I freak out," I ask her, my hands starting to shake. These vamps could kill us, or even worse, torture us. They might only collect young women for reasons I can't even imagine. Oh my god, vampires are real. They are real, and I've been kidnapped by them, bitten by them, and I'm likely never to go home. Never see my parents again.

What if they have my brother? What if they have killed him?

She is silent for a second or two, letting me freak out before she clicks her fingers, getting my attention. "It's normal to have a panic attack or ten. Try breathing slowly and counting to ten. Then count to twenty. And so on."

I do as she asks, even when it feels like each breath hurts more than the last, but I say each of the numbers. Eventually I calm down enough to rest back, my hands still shaking, but I don't feel seconds away from passing out anymore.

"My name is Riona Dark, and my friends call me Ria. What's your name?" I eventually question. We are stuck here together, we might as well get to know each other.

"Ann Hellerud," she replies, and I wish I could see what she looks like, to have some connection to normality out here. But it's too dark, I can only make out the shape of her head when she moves and maybe dark brown hair. "And, Ria, I hope we survive whatever is coming next."

"Same," I whisper back, though my voice carries

across the room. "Do you have a family? Someone who would be looking for you?"

"Two little brothers and my dad," she replies, and I can hear the affection in her voice. "I was the first one in my family to go to university, and I wanted to get a good job, show my brothers they could do it. My mum died a few years back from cancer, and she so desperately wanted me to make a difference in the world. So I was going to be a social worker, help anyone I could. Now..."

"You will get back to university," I firmly reply, though I have no way to make that happen, but it doesn't harm anyone to hope. Hope might be what gets us through this. She is a strong person, I can tell from her voice alone. "Just like I will find my brother and somehow escape whatever these vampires want with us. Did you hear them say anything that might give us a clue?"

"Yes...," she admits, but that fear is back in her voice. "They said something about auctions and food. I think they are going to sell us to other vampires."

"Fuck," I mutter under my breath, and I close my eyes, resting my head back. "I'm not being some vamp's long-term snack, that's for sure."

Ann doesn't reply to me, not that I blame her, as

the mood is sour at best now. I stare up at the top of the ceiling, through slight gaps in the panels of wood, and I can make out the moon and stars in the sky. I shiver from the cold as my eyes drift shut, and sleep soon lulls me into a false sense of safety.

"Time to get them up!" I hear a man bellow outside the room we are in, many days later from when we were taken. The cold has well and truly seeped into my bones, and I'm clueless how Ann and I are still alive and not dead from frostbite. Ann mentioned that the blood taste in our mouths might mean they gave us vampire blood, and perhaps it is somehow keeping us alive and healthy. I prefer not to over-think on that subject. Other than throwing bottled water and stale bread at us, this is the first time we are actually going to leave the room, by the sounds of it. A part of me is excited as much as I am terrified. The ship is still rocking slightly, but it seems less harsh now, and I wonder if we are anchored somewhere.

The door swings open, and a bulky man with green eyes, dark tanned skin, and a mixture of tattoos all up his chest and arms looks in at us with a flashlight, the light filling the room. The rapid change in light makes my eyes water and sting to hold open, but I force myself to. His clothes are old fashioned and remind me of what a pirate in a fairy-tale book might wear, and he looks between the other girls and me. Getting a good look at my new friend, I see she does have long dark brown hair and slightly tanned skin with tattoos down her arms from her shoulders. With only cut-off denim jeans and a white tank top that is covered in her blood, she must be as freezing as me. I hear dozens of other footsteps nearby, more doors opening, and the distant sound of the ocean waves as Ann's wide brown eyes fall on me before we both look at the vamp, who lets out a long sigh.

"Ladies don't like to wear much clothing anymore, do they? Not like in my time, with the big dresses," he states, disgust and pity in his voice. He lowers the flashlight in his hand.

What century are these vamps from?

The man doesn't say another word as he eventually walks in and goes to Ann first. Even in the darkness, which I'm now realising these vamps must be able to see in, I hear Ann's relief as the man undoes the cuffs, and they fall to the floor. I can't wait to get mine off; they are digging harshly into the skin on my wrists, and I think they are bleeding a little bit.

"Behave or you will regret it," the man warns, his accent very unfamiliar to me the more he talks. It almost sounds Scottish, but it's not, and I'm unsure where I've heard it before. Ann and I don't reply to that threat, mostly because what can you say?

I'm hardly going to enthusiastically say yes and be a good little girl, now am I? The man undoes my cuffs next, and instantly I sigh at the relief as I rub my sore wrists, feeling the cuts and bruises those cuffs left as I stand up next to Ann. I place my hand on my neck, running my fingers over the two bite marks I find there and the dried blood stuck to me even though it's been days.

The man shoves me hard in the middle of my back, and I stumble out into the corridor, the light hurting my eyes from the fire sconces lining the walls. Eventually, I settle my eyes and look to Ann, who staggers to my side, her arm brushing against mine. I've never seen her around the university, but it's a hella big university, and I would guess she is a first-year anyway, as she looks younger than me but not by much. I never thought to ask her age in the days we have been trapped here. In fact, we haven't spoken much about anything serious or real.

"Keep moving!" the man shouts behind me, and I trip with my bare feet across the wooden floorboards, almost slipping on some of the wet parts until I get to stairs at the end. I climb up them, hearing screams behind me that make the situation so much more petrifying. I've always been a strong person, and I don't intend to let this break me. But it's hard not to scream, to not freak the hell out. Every step feels like I'm walking to my death, and I likely am doing just that. I wrap my arms around myself, my pink dress doing nothing to curb the sheer cold wind as I step out onto the deck of a ship, my feet sticking to the deck panels, and into the crowd of people dressed in party clothes and smothered with blood. A few of them are openly weeping on the floor, others are shaking from the cold and huddled together. I can't hear much over the weeping and the sound of the sea, and the odd laugh from the vampires at the front of the group, talking together. The ship is a mixture of old and new, by the looks of it, with old floor-boards and a glass top above us, stopping the pouring rain from soaking us to the bone. There are modern lights on the sides of the walls, and overall, I'm more freaked out than ever.

But as much as the ship is distracting, it's nothing compared to the island in front of me in the distance. Even at night...I know this place is nothing like anywhere on earth. Or nothing I've ever seen before.

Three mountains tower into the sky in the middle of the island, disappearing into the clouds, and red snow pours down them like a fog, moving softly. Around the mountains is a vibrant city, and I can just make out the many, many lights of the buildings. The edges of the island look like thick forests, and one side seems to have beaches and the other just sheer cliffs. Several ships, like the one we are on, line the harbour of the beach, and I can see piles of people being herded like cattle into the forest line off the beach.

Ann moves close to my side, her arm hooking into mine as she stares with me at the vampire pirate things. I'm no geography student, but I know this place isn't on any human map, but then again, I hardly got kidnapped by a human. These are vampires, and it doesn't surprise me they have a secret island to live on. Not one thing about them could pass as human. They are too perfect, too shiny, and they stand too still. Humans are flawed and imperfect, something these monsters are not.

And I honestly think we are the winners. Being flawed is what makes us human.

"Welcome to The Onyx, the island of vampires and many, many human slaves," one of the vamps shouts out, stepping in front of us all and clapping his hands. The crying and weeping doesn't stop, it only gets louder. I search the humans, so many of them, for my brother, Sophie, Arlo or anyone I recognise, but I just can't see them all in this group. There must be a hundred people, easily. My brother could be here, and unless I move around, which might piss off the vamps and end with my head being torn off, I can't see him.

Onyx. This island has a name and a whole race of supernatural beings that belong in movies and TV shows. Not real life.

"This is your home now, and you will be looked after if you behave. The Onyx has a saying, and you will do well to listen to it. There is no power in The Onyx except for blood and death."

Ann looks at me, and I carefully hide my fear, knowing it's pointless to make her more afraid. I have a bad feeling blood is the only reason we are here. The vampires need food, and we are just cattle they have rounded up. "You have two of the most coveted things on The Onyx. Blood and the ability to die. But make no mistake, from now on, you are a slave to your masters, and if you wish to survive, you must follow the rules. We aren't all that bad."

"Bullshit," I whisper to Ann, who nods with a

little tilt of her lips. But they want us to act like sheep? Then fine.

At least until they realise the sheep aren't all the same, and there is a wolf here waiting to bite back. I'm not going down without a hell of a fight, that's for sure, but first I want to make sure my brother isn't on this goddamn island with me. Or Arlo or Sophie for that matter. Part of me suspects Sophie is okay, but Austin and Arlo? I'm not too sure. The vamp seems done with his shit speech and clicks his fingers. The other vamps start grabbing the people near the front and pulling them with them to the end of the ship, and they climb down into awaiting boats, I assume.

The one vamp, who I recognise from the beach, searches the crowd until he finds me. With dark tousled hair, muck-covered skin littered with scars, and almost black eyes, he is hard to forget. I only saw him briefly, but he is memorable. I know when he finds me as he walks through the screaming group, who part quickly, and he stops close so I'm forced to smell his dirty clothes. God, he stinks. Do vamps not need to shower? He reaches out, cupping the back of my neck and pulling me to him, turning my head to the side. I smack my hands against his chest, trying to pull away, but he is too strong. He doesn't even notice my efforts.

"I will buy you and keep you, pet," he coos, leaning down and pressing his nose into my neck before lifting his head. "I can still taste your sweet blood on my tongue. You smell like the angels themselves sent you here."

I sneer at him, even when I know it will get me nowhere, but I won't let him bite me again. "Your friend said in The Onyx there is no power but blood and death, so that means my biggest power is my blood and my decision when to die. I would rather kill myself than be your plaything."

He laughs and it's bitter, cruel. "Who says you get to die in The Onyx?"

"I do," I bite out.

He leans closer, and I try to fight his grip on me once again. "No, you don't. Your freedom is gone, but keep fighting me; I do like it when my prey fights back."

I scream and try to hit him, but he picks me up like a doll and carries me to the edge of the ship before dropping me. I scream as I fall and land harshly on my side, hearing something snap in my arm. I cry out as hands pick me up and pull me down to sit as I cup my arm, trying not to cry. But tears fall down my cheeks as I look up, seeing the bastard vampire who bit me looking down from the ship.

Bastard. Before I die, I'm finding out how to kill vampires and taking as many of them as I can down with me. I turn away, knowing he will keep staring, and the sick freak probably likes the attention. I glance around me, seeing a large wooden motorized boat full of people hiding in every corner of the boat but Ann is not one of them. The engine starts up, and I look up at the vampire who bit me and dragged me here.

He is going to die before I do, even if it's the last thing I do. Everyone has a weakness, and I bet vampires aren't all that different.

Either way, I'm not going down without a fight.

Chapter Thirty

I t's cold. Not that annoying sort of cold, but
the temperature that worries me that frostbite
is a real issue, and I like my toes where they
are. The vamps don't seem to give a monkey's arse
about us as we walk through the red snow covering
the sand, away from the docked boat. My clothes are
still wet, and it is odd they don't care about keeping
us alive, considering all they went through to kidnap
us. Maybe they do this a lot, and it's not odd at all. I
think of my uncle for a moment...he was right. He
said they were out hunting, and he was dead bang
right about it all. *But how could he have known that?*

The dock was empty, with nothing more than a
rocky, snow-covered beach and a few trees to be seen
after we got out of the boat. There are twenty-four of

us in this group—I counted on the boat—and three vamps. I don't know what I expected, but it wasn't the silence of the island in the dead of the night. The forest seems endless, as does the snow freezing my toes off, until we come to a house in the middle of it. The house appears normal, nothing odd about it at all, but it feels all kinds of wrong. The house itself is attached to the bottom of the mountain, and its white-framed windows and brick walls look almost out of place here. There is nothing personalised about the house, and soon the vamp opens the door, and we are ushered inside.

All of us are crammed into this tiny house, and I wonder if there are others like it? There was certainly more than one ship. I consider running away for a brief second...but then the thought comes...where would I go?

How am I going to escape this damn island?

I follow the guy in front of me into the house, which is warm, and my toes are thankful for it as I stand shivering in the hallway, nothing but several doors and a staircase to look at.

"Send one of them up!" a woman shouts down, her very British and almost Cockney, aka London-sounding, voice familiar to my ears. Please pick someone else. Please pick—I'm jolted from my thoughts as a vamp man grabs my elbow and leads me to the stairs, giving me a slight shove up the first two steps.

Pushing down my fear, I walk to the top of the stairs, which opens to one massive room littered with four wardrobes and two dressing tables. Shelves of boxes fill the corner of the room, and there are several white doors. The house creaks in the wind, and it smells like expensive perfume in here.

A woman stands in the middle of the room, and I stare at her as she looks right back. She is pretty and strange all at the same time. With her long black hair, dark tanned skin, and stylish brown leather dress, she almost seems normal, but then I see the tattoos on her cheeks. Two sigils, if I guess right, and they are completely different. One is a circle shape with birds making the circle, and in the middle is a sword with wings behind it. The other one is a dragon wrapped around a dagger with fire in a circle around it. They look burnt on, like she was branded many years ago, as they are fully healed. Why would anyone do that to themselves?

I don't know how I know it, but this woman is a vamp. I think it's the way they hold themselves, no crouching or movements like breathing. She is just still, and the more she stares, the more uncomfortable I get, but I still hold eye contact. Her sharp green eyes are a clear challenge.

"Oh, they will like you, girl," she eventually states, breathing out the sentence in a husky tone. "I can smell your blood from here, and it is different. Delicious."

She licks her lips. "I might bid for you myself, seeing as I'm not allowed to feed on the new stock."

"Were you ever human?" I question, crossing my arms. I'm done being frightened of these monsters if they are going to kill me anyway. "Are you all born vampires with no ounce of humanity left to save you?"

She laughs and walks across the room. "Humanity is overrated, as are your emotions that come with it."

I don't reply, unsure what to say to that. Humanity would be overrated to someone who clearly has none. "But humans are as cruel as we are, make no mistake about that. The Onyx owns its crimes and doesn't hide them. Can you say the same of your race? How many terrible things have you humans done and hid?"

"Why am I here?" I question instead, hating that she might be right.

"To prepare you. I will run you a bath and dress

you, and then you will be taken. It is the way of things around here," she casually comments. "My name is Merethe."

"My mum always said it was rude to play with your food. Why don't you just kill me and get it over and done with?" I ask her instead of giving her my name.

She tilts her head to the side. "Do you want to die? Is there no one you want to go back to?"

"My family would rather see me dead than in constant suffering," I counter.

She leans down close, shaking her head. "Not everything in The Onyx is about suffering. Pleasure is just as much a desire as blood is. Both can be enjoyed at the same time. You will see, you are very beautiful."

I turn away, sickness filling my mouth. That is a fate worse than death in my books. "I will be no one's."

She laughs like that is impossible here. "Are you a virgin?"

"What does that matter to you?" I snap. She keeps laughing and steps close to me so quickly I can't track her movement. Her hand cups my face, and her eyes stare into mine. "Tell me the truth, are you a virgin?"

Something indescribable takes hold of me, forcing me to want to tell her the truth, but I push it back, gritting my teeth. It hurts to resist, and the more she stares at me, the more pressure I feel until it suddenly disappears. "Fuck. Off."

Shock fills her eyes, and she lets me go, stumbling back. "How...how did you do that?"

"Do what?" I question, not understanding how freaked out she is. Rather than answer me, she starts to pace, muttering to herself, and I catch some of it.

"Must tell...princes...they will pay more."

Princes? Don't tell me the vamps have a royal family.

"Hello?" I wave my hand, and she finally stops, plastering on a very fake smile and breathing out a long breath. Her eyes stare me down like I'm a prized pig at a Texas BBQ.

"Let's get you dressed up. You look cold," she replies, pretending like our whole conversation didn't just happen, but she looks at me differently now than when I first came in here. It's almost like I suddenly turned into gold. "Everything will be better once you are warm and dressed in auction house clothes of a neutral colour. Can't have any arguments about you that are blamed on me."

"Why does the colour matter?" I question,

holding my ground. She walks away and into another room, and I stand still, wondering if I should follow her. Every inch of me wants to run away as fast as I can, but I know running isn't going to work well for me until I come up with a decent enough plan.

My brother always said I was the smart one of us both. And he was damn right.

Steeling my back, I keep my arms crossed as I walk to the room Merethe last went into and head inside. It's a small bathroom with a white tub, a modern one with its own shower head. Merethe is running the steamy water into the tub and pouring something that smells like lavender in.

"Get undressed," she commands and pauses to look at me. "Not that you're wearing much to begin with," she tuts. "Humans."

I scowl at her as she turns back, and I awkwardly stand there, not wanting to get undressed in front of her. Merethe sighs, turns the tap off, and comes to me.

"Nudity is not a care for vampires or d'vampires on this island," she firmly tells me and grips my dress. In one smooth motion, she rips it off me, and I gasp at the slight pain that caused. I cover my bra-clad breasts and panties with my hands, and she rolls her eyes at me. "You can keep them on if you like."

"Yes," I answer and tip toe my way to the tub. I climb in, my feet stinging from the sheer difference in heat and the tiny cuts I can feel on the base of them. Sitting still, I nearly jump when Merethe leans over me, grabs the shower head, and turns it on. She washes my hair like we are old friends, pouring in shampoo and conditioner by the feel and smell, and I just sit there. I feel numb. Shocked into staying still.

"What is the difference between vampires and d'vampires?" I question, needing to understand the creatures on this island more if I have any chance of surviving this.

She sighs. "Vampires are born, like humans are, and d'vampires are humans who have been turned. D'vampires cannot turn humans, but they are just as strong as born vampires. Honestly, there is not much difference."

"When can I go home?" I quietly ask. Merethe turns the shower off and squeezes out the water from my hair before stepping back. I look up, meeting her eyes, and I see some pity there.

"Most ask that first, and then they freak out when I answer them," she comments, her voice lacking human emotion of any kind. "Then they threaten to kill themselves, which some do anyway, or they try to run. Running gets you nowhere, by the way. I was surprised you didn't ask any of these questions."

"How do you keep us under control then?" I ask.

"Compulsion, plain and simple. Compulsion is my art, I am the best at it, and that's why I see the humans first and...soothe them," she replies with a smirk. "And you're the first human I've ever seen resist it. Are you sure you're not a witch or something else?"

"Are witches real?" I question back, my mouth popping open. Vampires are bad enough. Witches? Nope. I still remember that film I watched as a kid where the witches turned kids into mice. I shiver. Standing out from the other humans was not the game plan. I need to go unnoticed to escape, and I have a sinking feeling that isn't happening here. What is wrong with me? I should have just pretended to do what she asked.

"Very real and dangerous. But you can't be one; you don't have the markings, and you are human. I smell it," she replies and offers me a towel before turning around as I take it off her. I wrap myself up and climb out, the cold air brushing against my skin. "Get changed into that dress and blow dry your hair over there. Don't do anything rash, I am listening. We vampires have excellent hearing."

With that, she walks out of the room and leaves me alone. I walk over to the small dressing table with a hair dryer, a small and old one by the looks of it, and a weird brown dress hanging up nearby on the wall. The dress is more of a sari with woven feathers all at the base of the dress, and it's made from soft silk in three different shades of brown. It feels expensive under my fingers, and I hate that. I'm a prisoner, nothing more, and now I'm being dressed up for them to ogle. It takes me more than a few attempts to get the dress on and to work out that the design of the dress leaves my shoulders free and is tight around my waist.

Which makes sense with the whole biting of the neck thing. They wouldn't want fabric in the way.

I quickly blow dry my hair and brush the knots out before standing up, looking at myself in the small foggy mirror.

I don't look like me. I feel like the person in the mirror has aged a million years in only a few days. The beach, the party and my innocence seem like an old memory. My eyes catch the water in the tub, seeing it has turned pink from my dried blood.

I don't think pink is going to be my colour

anymore…it seems like blood red might be the colour I need to get used to. Cooling my shaky hands by plastering them to my sides, I walk out still in bare feet to the main area. Merethe turns around and smiles.

"You remind me of my first day here," she comments, her eyes fixated on me. Something changes as she looks away and points at three boxes by the wall. "Take any shoes you like and meet me down these stairs. Be quick."

She disappears before my eyes, and I only hear the creak of a floor panel to let me know she went that way. So the vampires can move fast, and Merethe was once human. More things to figure out later. If I manage to survive.

Peeling myself from where I was standing, I walk to the boxes and pull the lid off the first. It takes me a little while to find any shoes that fit my tiny UK size four feet, but eventually I find some worn leather boots. I slide them on, grimacing at the feeling of the leather against my cut feet without socks. I stand up and fix my eyes on a shelf above the boxes and what looks like a knife resting on the edge. Quickly, I put the lid back on the box and stand on it, reaching up and skimming my fingers across the edge of the shelf until I grab the blade handle. I pull it down, smiling to myself about my little find. The knife is sharp, and it has a black leather handle—nothing special, but it might get me out of here. I tuck the knife into my dress, using the many layers of fabric to secure it to my chest.

Feeling a little less nervous, I go to the stairs and walk down to the bottom, finding the place full of people sitting on the floor and Merethe waiting for me. She instantly grabs my upper arm and starts dragging me through the house until we get to a metal gate. Merethe places her hand on it, and it glows red for a second before the gate opens, revealing row after row of cages which are full of people, their desperate eyes cutting into me. Then I hear the screams and cries, the pleas that echo around the place.

"W-what was that?" I whisper.

Merethe laughs. "Witches built this island, and vampires took it, keeping every little spell they ever did. Welcome to your new life, Riona Dark. I have a feeling you won't be leaving any time soon."

Chapter Thirty-One

All night, there are screams. Screams of people who want to escape, screams of people in pain, and so many different types it's impossible to do anything but listen. The screams are worse than the cries and pleas for help, for death, for anything or anyone to save them. My cage is a damp brick room with holes in many places, rat droppings in every corner, and one large arched metal gate with thick iron bars. The ceiling is pure stone but littered with tiny holes, and in the middle, there is a dim lightbulb on its own, every so often flickering. Even if I could somehow reach up, I doubt the broken glass of a lightbulb would help me much as a weapon. There are four other women in here with me, and we each sit in our own space, no one saying a word.

Because what is there to say? We all know we are screwed.

I do notice all the women must be under twenty-five, and they are all wearing brown clothes like I am, but theirs don't seem to be as nice as mine. Basically, I somewhat stand out compared to them, and I don't like that. Morning light flickers in even as my eyes threaten to close, but my body is awake, too wired up to rest. Three of the other girls here are fast asleep, two blondes and a black-haired woman. The only other person awake sits still, her gaze empty as she stares at nothing.

"Hi," I say, as lame as it is. The girl doesn't move or react, it's almost like I'm talking to a ghost. I try again. "Hello?"

"Don't bother, she has been here longer than any of us, and she doesn't talk. They cut out her tongue and used their blood to stop her bleeding," one of the blondes speaks up. I turn to look at her, her tanned skin and accent making me think she is from California, or near enough. There was a family that moved to my town when I was seven, and they were from California, moved for work. "What's your name, and where you from?"

"Riona Dark, and I'm from Aberdeen, well, a village nearby it. I was taken from my university," I loosely explain. Talking about the beach, the fact my brother and friends might be here and hurt, is too raw. I clear my throat. "What about you?"

"Lucy Denlake," she replies cheerily, but I suspect that is just her nature coming through. "And I lived in a beach house in California. Damn, they took us from thousands of miles apart. Look, these girls don't speak, or they are shit scared, but you seem like me. You've accepted your bad luck, and I think that might mean we are more likely to survive. Can you promise me something, and I will do the same for you if you want?"

"Why not?" I answer. I know I shouldn't be making promises to strangers, but what could the harm be?

"If you escape this place, hopefully killing a few vamps on the way out, will you tell my boyfriend that I love him and have since third grade? His name is Rowan, and he will be looking for me in California. It shouldn't be too hard to find him on Facebook or something," she replies, breathing out a long exhale of cold air. "Do you have someone you want me to tell something to if I get out?"

I stare at her for a moment, seeing the desperation in her eyes.

"My brother is here somewhere, I'm sure of it...but my parents—" I gulp. "You could tell them I love them, and tell my uncle I wish I had listened to his letter," I whisper, looking away at the floor. "I promise to pass on your message if I can."

"Same," she softly replies, and I look up, meeting her eyes. We both smile a little. "And if Rowan doesn't believe you, tell him that tattoo on my butt is our secret. He will then."

I chuckle a little. "What's the tattoo of?"

She laughs and shakes her head. "You'll never know."

I laugh with her, and then I hear footsteps nearby, close enough to be heard over the distant screams and cries. Two pairs of them, and never before have I feared the sound of someone walking towards me as much as I do right now. I stand up, as does Lucy. The other girls all cower together in the corner, and Lucy moves to stand in front of them. I place my hand on the dagger under my dress, knowing it has to be the right time to use and not a second too soon. If one of these assholes tries to bite me, I can at least stab them and see if they bleed.

"Here is that one Merethe talked about," an

Irish-sounding man states and chuckles after he speaks. "Though Merethe might be going senile. I doubt she is as great as she made out, sir. Maybe she is losing her touch."

There is silence for a reply for a long while. Tension fills the cell, even when they aren't inside it. When he speaks, his voice seems to suck the light from the room, and his dark, deep and cold voice takes over it. "Open the door and leave."

I shiver from the sheer coldness and power in that voice that unsettles me right down to my core. A man in an old suit, with a pocket watch hanging out of his pocket, steps in front of the metal cage to the door, pulling out keys from his brown trouser pockets. He has grey hair that matches his bushy grey beard, but there is no doubt he isn't human. He quickly opens the metal cage door and steps back, though his eyes fall on me for a moment.

My heart pounds as a man walks into the room and stops. I know for certain he is the one who spoke, he is the one that I should fear.

He is six foot easily, towering over me, and he is gorgeous in a way that can only be described as inhuman.

Immortal.

And so *very* not human. Sharp black eyebrows

rest above his dark eyes. He has thick brown, almost black hair that falls around his face and stops at his shoulders. Several strands have been braided with red crystals, and silver rings clipped into the braids catch the sunlight. His jawline could make any god weep in its perfection, and his narrow lips seem soft almost, even with a light scruff of a beard gracing his jawline. His cheekbones are high and look strong enough to cut glass, and everything about him seems...cold. Empty. Lost.

Then his dark eyes lock onto mine, and I suck in a deep mouthful of air. Dark is a small word to describe his eyes, which are half black and half a deep red, the colour of blood. The black and red mixes together effortlessly, and it's memorizing to stare at.

"Come to me," he commands, and it's a command mixed with magic, to say the least. Whatever the magic is, it pushes into me like a storm against a shore, and it hurts. God, it hurts to stop it taking over me. I grit my teeth through the pain, refusing to cower, refusing to back down. The seconds tick on and on until he stops and walks right up to me, grabbing my chin. His nails are sharp and completely black, curved into points that dig into my skin.

"Will you scream if I sink my teeth into your pretty neck and drain all of that courage right out of you?" he almost purrs. "Will you scream my name and beg me to stop?"

"Considering I don't know your name, it's unlikely. Unless you like being called Bastard, in which case, I can definitely call you that," I growl right back at him, even as his grip borders on painful.

He could hurt me if he wanted. He could break me.

The vampire's eyes widen with what I think is amusement and shock. "I will buy you and keep you as mine. Mine to bite, mine to fuck, and mine in fucking general. Get used to the idea."

"I'd rather die," I bite back.

His eyes narrow, and he digs his nails into my skin, enough to make several cuts. He drops me quickly, and my back scratches across the wall as I fall, managing to stop myself tumbling onto my ass. Damn. Effing. Vampires. My blood coats his nails as he slowly licks each one, his eyes closed shut, but I think he likes what he tastes.

One of the girls behind Lucy makes a small noise, and the vampire swiftly turns towards them, noticing they are there for the first time. He moves quicker than I can track, and then he has Lucy in his arms, and she screams as he bites into her neck. I don't know how long I stare, paralyzed on the spot in fear as he drains her, but her screams slowly fade, and eventually her body goes limp before he lets her drop to the floor.

"Riona Dark, I will enjoy your company and your blood, I'm sure," the vampire tells me, walking to the cage door like nothing happened and he didn't just kill someone. He is fucking insane. "My name is Prince Maddox Borealis of the Vampires, and everyone calls me the Mad Prince."

I stay silent as he leaves, never looking back once, and the second the gate shuts, I fall to my knees and throw up everything in my system, which isn't much more than stale bread and water. After I stop heaving, I break into sobs, which I stop escaping my lips by holding my hand over my mouth. Tears fall down my cheeks endlessly as I resist the urge to scream and scream. Crawling over the stone floor, I pick up Lucy's head off the ground and brush some of the hair from her eyes, her vacant eyes that stare up at nothing above me.

My mum's words come to haunt me as I close Lucy's eyes and say a silent prayer. "When everyone dies, they look at peace. So there is no need to fear what comes after death, because I have seen it is a better place than life. You may rest and god will watch over you. You're with the angels now."

Of course, she doesn't reply, and it doesn't make me feel better, but I hope she heard me somewhere. I close her eyes shut, giving her the peace she deserves, before resting my forehead against hers.

"I hope you're at peace, Lucy Denlake, and I will keep my promise," I whisper to her. The three other girls never move from the wall, and one starts screaming not long after, the screams mixing with those in the distance.

Hope is an easy thing to squash, apparently. All you need is death.

Printed by Amazon Italia Logistica S.r.l.
Torrazza Piemonte (TO), Italy

36160748R00169